Heartwood Hotel

BETTER TOGETHER

Also by Kallie George

Heartwood Hotel, Book 1: A True Home

Heartwood Hotel, Book 2: The Greatest Gift

The Magical Animal Adoption Agency, Book 1: Clover's Luck

The Magical Animal Adoption Agency, Book 2: The Enchanted Egg

The Magical Animal Adoption Agency, Book 3: The Missing Magic

Heartwood Hotel

BETTER TOGETHER

Kallie George

illustrated by
Stephanie Graegin

LITTLE, BROWN AND COMPANY
New York Boston

Text copyright © 2018 by Kallie George
Illustrations copyright © 2018 by Stephanie Graegin

Cover illustration copyright © 2018 by Stephanie Graegin. Cover design by Phil Caminiti. Cover copyright © 2018 by Hachette Book Group, Inc.

Little, Brown and Company
Hachette Book Group
1290 Avenue of the Americas, New York, NY 10104
Visit us at LBYR.com

Originally published in hardcover, trade paperback, and ebook by Disney • Hyperion, an imprint of Disney Book Group, in February 2018
First Edition: February 2018

Little, Brown and Company is a division of Hachette Book Group, Inc.
The Little, Brown name and logo are trademarks of Hachette Book Group, Inc.

Library of Congress Cataloging-in-Publication Data
Names: George, Kallie, author | Graegin, Stephanie, illustrator.
Title: Better together / by Kallie George ; illustrated by Stephanie Graegin.
Description: First edition. | Los Angeles ; New York : Disney/HYPERION, 2018. | Series: Heartwood Hotel ; 3 | Summary: Spring is here and the animal staff at the Heartwood Hotel are busy arranging a series of festivals and competitions to drum up business and to show its patrons that Heartwood is the greatest hotel in Fernwood Forest.
Identifiers: LCCN 2016054240 | ISBN 9781484732359 (hardcover) | ISBN 1484732359 (hardcover)
Subjects: CYAC: Hotels, motels, etc.—Fiction. | Forest animals—Fiction. | Spring—Fiction.
Classification: LCC PZ7.G293326 Be 2018 • DDC [Fic]—dc23
LC record available at https://lccn.loc.gov/2016054240

ISBNs: 978-1-484-74640-0 (pbk.), 978-1-484-74738-4 (ebook)

Printed in the United States of America

LSC-C

Printing 5, 2021

For Tiff
—K.G.

For Kristina and Kayley
—S.G.

Contents

1: Mr. Heartwood Heads Off 1

2: Cleaning and Clues 8

3: Brumble Brings News 19

4: The Spring Splash 28

5: The Ruffled Robinsons 36

6: The Cutest Egg Competition 44

7: The Tiniest Talent Show 58

8: The Best Blossom Contest 73

9: Skim the Snail 86

10: A Tiff with Tilly 99

11: Mona's Moment 110

12: Darkness Descends 118

13: Better Together 124

14: Firefly Works 136

15: Mona Mends 145

16: The Heartwood Hop 153

1

MR. HEARTWOOD HEADS OFF

There was a buzz in the air at the Heartwood Hotel. Mona the mouse could feel it in her whiskers. It was spring, and the guests, staff, and even the tree itself were beginning to buzz with activity. Buds were bursting on the branches, sap seeped from the bark, and the floors had a bounce to them. There was even a *real* buzz, too: from the bees, who had been hired to make honey for the guests.

The only one who wasn't full of energy was Mr. Heartwood, the hotel's owner. Winter had been unusually eventful, and the great

1

badger had been dragging his paws ever since. So, at last, with much encouragement from everyone, he was going to take a break and visit a friend.

All the staff were gathered in the lobby to see him off. It was like check-out—a really grand one.

Mona smoothed her maid's apron, making sure to look presentable, and straightened the key around her neck.

For once, Mr. Heartwood wasn't wearing his own keys or his vest. Instead, he sported a cardigan and a cap. Beside him was his suitcase, made of a burl with roots for handles. Mona had seen all sorts of suitcases in the hotel, from tiny seeds to hollow branches. His was the biggest.

But Mr. Heartwood wasn't picking it up. He was still trying to run the hotel.

"Is the spring cleaning . . ."

"Sorted and started, Mr. Heartwood," said Mrs. Higgins, the hedgehog head housekeeper.

"And the food . . ."

"Stocked and stored, Mr. Heartwood. We just got a shipment," said Ms. Prickles, the porcupine cook.

"What of bookings . . ."

"We're low so far this season—" started Mrs. Higgins.

"But don't worry," interrupted Gilles, the front-desk lizard. He would be in charge while Mr. Heartwood was away. "The Hop is coming, and I have plans to spruce it up."

"What's the Hop?" Mona whispered to Tilly.

"A big party—sort of like the Acorn Festival," Tilly the squirrel whispered back.

Tilly was not only Mona's best friend, but also the head maid, as well as the best grumper in the whole of the Heartwood. But lately she'd been grinning more than grumping, ever since she'd found Henry, her long-lost little brother.

"I love parties!" said Henry loudly. Henry had a *very* loud voice.

Mr. Heartwood didn't seem bothered. He smiled fondly at the squirrel. "I almost forgot. Here." Mr. Heartwood unclipped his suitcase and pulled out an acorn, handing it to Henry. "It's a Heartwood seed to toss and play, while I am with a friend . . ." He paused, searching for a rhyme. Mr. Heartwood always rhymed.

This time, though, Henry finished for him. "Thanks, Mr. Heartwood! Look!" he said to Mona and Tilly, extra loudly.

"Sh!" said Tilly. "We can play later."

Mr. Heartwood closed his suitcase and continued, "And what of safety . . ."

"No worries there, Mr. Heartwood," said Tony, the security woodpecker.

He winked at Mona.

Mona's whiskers straightened proudly. She might be a maid, but she had also saved the hotel, twice now, from wolves in the fall and hunger in the winter.

"Good. There's nothing to fear, not with all of you . . ." Mr. Heartwood struggled for a rhyme again. He usually had no trouble rhyming.

"There, there," said Ms. Prickles. "You best be off. You're not yourself at all. You really do need a rest."

"Indeed," said Mr. Heartwood. "Though my friend often has big plans of his own." He adjusted his cap and picked up his suitcase. "Remember: 'Sleep in safety, eat in earnest, and . . .'"

"'Be happy at the Heartwood!'" everyone chorused.

"Happiest!" said Gilles, turning a slightly brighter shade of green. "I will make sure of it."

Me too, thought Mona. "Good—" she started.

But Henry was faster. "Good-bye, Mr. Heartwood! GOOD-BYE!"

Through the open door, Mona watched Mr. Heartwood disappear into Fernwood Forest. *He*

won't be gone long, she thought. *What could possibly happen?*

Of course, this was the Heartwood Hotel, and you never knew what a season might bring.

CLEANING AND CLUES

"Bring that honey! And be quick! Be sharp! Be in line!" buzzed Captain Ruby, who preferred "captain" to "queen." "You know the rules." Mona heard the squadron of bees now, flying down the stairs to the kitchen.

No matter the rules, Ruby and her bees had gotten everything sticky. Their honey *was* delicious, but the mess it made added to the already long list of spring cleaning.

Which Mona and Tilly were *supposed* to be doing now that Mr. Heartwood had left. But Tilly had other plans.

"This way," she said, leading Mona away from the stairs and down a hall.

"What about cleaning the storage room?" asked Mona.

"This will only take a moment. Trust me—it's worth it." Tilly grinned.

They had arrived at the end of the hall. The squirrel pointed up.

"I don't see anything," said Mona.

"Look closer," said Tilly.

There on the hall ceiling, like a tiny star, hung a golden drop. The drop slipped, fell, and—*drip*—landed in a bowl. The bowl was filled with honey.

"It's coming from the hive, above. There's a crack in the floor," said Tilly. "I put the bowl there," she added.

"Should we tell Mrs. Higgins? Or Gilles? They could get the carpenter ants to fix it," started Mona.

"Fix it?" cried Tilly. "Who wants to fix it?!"

She produced two pine needles from her apron

pocket and handed one to Mona to swirl in the bowl. The honey stuck to it in a glob.

The honey *was* sweet and delicious, and Mona had to agree when Tilly licked her lips and said, "This is the way it should be. Honey's for eating, not cleaning."

"How did you find this?"

"I didn't. It was—"

"Me!" At that moment, down the hall burst none other than Henry, his tail almost as big as his body.

Tilly gave him an extra-big grin.

"I'm always finding good things like that,"

Henry said. "I've practically discovered EVERY secret room and passageway. It's my nose. I've got the BEST nose, you know," he bragged. "I smelled that you were here. Is it time for a break? Can we play? You promised."

"Not yet," said Tilly.

"Go on," said Mona, feeling generous. "I can finish up the storage room."

Mona watched as they bounded down the stairs together, one big red tail, one little, both equally bristly.

If any of Mona's family had been alive, she'd be taking a break with them, too. She didn't mind doing a little extra work for her friend.

But when Mona opened the last of the storage-room doors, she gulped. It wasn't a *little* extra cleaning. It was a *lot*!

The room was huge and a mess, stuffed with books, boxes, and even a bed! There was a tee-tering stack of umbrellas made of woven reeds, a

big dusty box of holly berry decorations, and an ancient trunk labeled ODDS AND ENDS.

Luckily, Mona felt up to the task—with the honey humming through her. She briskly swept the room with her dandelion broom, tidying as she went. She still couldn't dust with her tail like Tilly, but she'd been practicing straightening things with it, and she was getting better and better.

There was something satisfying about spring cleaning. Like putting on her perfectly pressed apron, the one that Tilly had made for her, with the heart. And something exciting, too, about going through old and new rooms that Mona had never seen before. It was less like cleaning and more like secret-finding.

Just as she thought that, she spied something.

Along one wall was a large bookshelf lined with birch-bark volumes, each with a heart on its spine. *What could these be?* Mona wondered.

Curious, she leaned her broom against the shelf and stood on tiptoe to pull one out.

The book was heavy for a mouse to lift. She nearly toppled over from its weight, but with difficulty she managed to carry it over and put it down, as carefully as she could, on the bed. When she opened the birch-bark cover, the pages were curled with age, but she could still read the entry.

We were so pleased to celebrate our wedding here. Apologies for the smell. We were simply both so nervous. But everything went according to plan. We look forward to returning for anniversaries henceforth.
—The Sudsburys

Mona knew the Sudsburys. She had prepared the honeymoon suite for the skunks when they were at the hotel in the fall, for their tenth wedding anniversary.

And now she knew what these books were, too.

The guest books! There was always one in the lobby for guests to fill out. She'd never thought about what happened to them once they were full. The guest books were where guests recorded their experiences at the hotel. She turned the page, wondering what other entries might say. The next one was a little hard to make out because of the spelling.

I am sory I ate the dornob. It wuʒ a gud mushroom but mummy sed no. I will lissen nex time. I promiss.
—Sally the skwirl

Mona giggled. Then she thought of Henry and sighed. Sally reminded her of Tilly's brother. Henry wouldn't eat a doorknob—he wasn't *that* young—but he *was* always getting in the way. She flipped a few pages forward.

What a humongous disaster! My doorknob was eaten, and my room smelled like skunks. Clearly living by "Protect and Respect," not by "Tooth

and Claw," isn't working at this hotel. If it hadn't been for the delicious nectar parfait, I would have left.
—Hyacinth the hummingbird

Mona's whiskers drooped. Poor Hyacinth. At least the food had helped. And pleased the next guest, too . . . or so it seemed.

Seedcakes warm, soufflés hot,
You'll be with me in my thoughts.
—Q

How mysterious. Mona wondered how many mysteries these books held, how many stories—all the way back to the hotel's beginning.

All the way back to . . . her parents!

Her parents had stayed for many months at the Heartwood. Although they had helped out, they hadn't been staff. They had been guests! Guests who might have written something in a *guest* book!

She didn't know much about them, only that her mother had baked seedcakes as buttery as Ms. Prickles's, and her father had carved the heart on the Heartwood Hotel's front door. Of course, that was long ago, before she was born, before they had lost their lives in a storm. Mona didn't have any brothers or sisters, only them. She'd always wanted to know more. Maybe this was her chance.

But then she glanced up at the books.

There were so many. Hundreds of little hearts, in row after row, filling the bookshelf. Some looked newer, some older. Where should Mona start?

It would take her forever to read them all. Unless she had help.

Tilly! Tilly could help her read them.

And so, after struggling to put the book back up on the shelf, Mona hurried out to find her friend and share her discovery. This was one time cleaning could wait.

After all, secrets were better shared, and friends were the best to share them with.

Brumble Brings News

The Heartwood Hotel door was a bit of a secret itself, with a lock that was carved like a heart that you pressed to open. It was hard to find on purpose, for safety. Every time Mona went in and out of the hotel, she thought of her dad. Finding a guest-book entry written by her parents would be even more special.

Mona stepped outside, but Tilly was too busy playing with Henry to notice her.

"Catch!" Tilly called to him.

Tilly and Henry were in front of the hotel, where the Heartwood grounds met the forest, partially

 19

hidden by one of the tree's huge roots. Mona could just see their ears and the tips of their tails, dancing back and forth.

"Good one!" shouted Tilly. An acorn ball soared up in the air and disappeared again.

Mona was just heading around the root when what Tilly said made her pause. "I've missed playing ball," Tilly continued. "There's no one like you to play with, Henry."

There's me, thought Mona.

Mona stepped out into the open.

"Catch!" Henry cried when he saw her.

Mona tried to, but the acorn ball was really big. It soared over her, hit the root, and rolled back, past Henry and off into the forest.

"You'd better go get that, Henry," said Tilly, shaking her head. She turned to Mona. "You're done already? That was fast!"

"Actually, no," said Mona. "But I want to tell you something."

 20

"There's something I wanted to talk to you about, too . . ." started Tilly.

But before either of them could say anything, there was a sharp cry. *"BZZT,* ATTACK!*"*

Captain Ruby's orders caused Mona and Tilly to jump—and Henry, too. He came running back without his acorn and hid behind his sister.

A buzzing formation of bees zigzagged above them, away from the Heartwood, right up to a giant black shape. A bear!

Not just any bear. Mona knew at once who this was: Brumble, a friend of the Heartwood. Even though he'd spent the last few months sleeping, not eating, it looked like he'd grown larger. His mountain of black fur seemed to have doubled, perhaps because it was sticking up here and there, in need of a good brush.

"Stop! Captain Ruby, stop!" Mona cried. Tilly and Henry had backed against the root, too scared to do anything.

 21

Brumble raised a front paw, looking more confused than angry. The bees split into two V formations, and Mona worried they were about to swarm.

"STOP!" Mona cried again, running closer. But Captain Ruby wasn't listening. Mona had to do something, before someone got hurt. What would a captain say? How did a captain say stop? "HALT!" she yelled.

It worked. Captain Ruby spun around midair to face Mona. "Miss Mouse, you must retreat! It's a bear!"

"And a friend!" said Mona.

Brumble, noticing Mona, put his paw down. "Friend," he said.

"Friend?" The captain looked astonished. "Bears aren't friends!"

"This one is," said Mona. "He helped save the hotel from the wolves in the fall."

"Did I?" Brumble asked in his gravelly voice.

 22

He didn't have the best memory. "Ah . . . yes." He smiled. "That's right. I've come to thank you for that honey you left for me, Mona. And to return this."

In his other paw, Mona now noticed he had a round pot, with HH carved on it. The Heartwood had left the pot filled with honey outside his den, as a thank-you for his help.

Captain Ruby looked taken aback. "So this is the bear I've heard stories of? My apologies, sir."

"Aw, shucks," said Brumble. "No sting, no need for a sorry."

"Very well, then," said the captain, "we'll be on our way. We have a leak to fix."

"There goes our drip," Mona heard Tilly grumble.

With that, Captain Ruby and her squadron gave a salute and flew back to their hive, in the huge hollow knot halfway up the tree.

"Gosh," said Brumble, "they fly quick. I'm just

glad I found the right place. I thought I had come to the other hotel."

"There's only one hotel in Fernwood, Brumble," said Mona, gently. "The Heartwood."

Brumble rubbed his nose. "Not anymore. There's a new hotel opening up. A splashy one."

"There is?" asked Mona.

"There isn't?" Brumble said.

Now Mona was as confused as he was.

"I heard it from some birds," said the bear. "I'm pretty sure I did. My memory IS better after my hibernation. But . . ."

GRRRR! There was a loud rumble. "Excuse me," said Brumble. "That's my stomach."

Suddenly he spotted an acorn—Henry's ball— near his paw. He licked it up and gave it a test crunch.

"Hey!" Henry cried, though he didn't budge from his place behind Tilly. "My toy! It was my present from Mr. Heartwood."

"Ooops!" said Brumble. He spat it out. The acorn was cracked.

"That's okay," said Mona. Actually, she was a little glad. Now she wouldn't have to deal with flying acorns anymore. But she was still confused. What was Brumble talking about? A new hotel?

GRRRR!

"I'd better go," said Brumble. "My stomach is bossy. It needs some berries."

After the big bear said his good-byes and bumbled on his way, Mona turned to Tilly and Henry.

Henry wasn't upset about his ball. He was excited. "I can't believe you just talked to a bear! You just went right up there. You are so brave, Mona! And can you believe what he said? A new hotel! A splashy one! We have to tell someone!"

"I don't know," said Mona. "Brumble's *got* to be confused."

"But what if he isn't?" said Tilly, matter-of-factly. "Henry's right, we should let Gilles know.

Besides, my stomach's grumbling, too. It's time for lunch."

Mona wasn't hungry. She was too full of thoughts. She gazed up at the Heartwood Hotel, with its majestic limbs and the tiny pinpricks of lights shining from the rooms like little stars.

She loved it so much. Was there really another hotel opening up in the forest? And if there was, what would that mean? She wasn't sure.

The hotel creaked as wind blew through its limbs, as though it wasn't sure either.

THE SPRING SPLASH

Mona and Tilly followed Henry downstairs into the kitchen, which was nestled between the Heartwood's roots.

The Heartwood Hotel had almost as many rooms below the earth as it did above. Mona loved them all, from the penthouse suite at the top, to the hibernation suites in the deep dirt. The kitchen was one of her favorite places.

It was the gathering place for staff, which was no surprise, since the air was always filled with delicious smells like roasting acorns and gooey cheese crumble. Ms. Prickles was always there, too, bustling about, baking up batch after batch of her famous seedcakes. Although you couldn't hug Ms. Prickles, she said she baked a hug into every one.

There didn't seem to be any hugs in the kitchen that lunchtime, though. Only crossed arms and tense tails.

Gilles, the front-desk lizard, was sitting in Mr. Heartwood's spot at the head of the table, wearing a badge with an *M* for manager on it.

Beside Gilles were Mrs. Higgins and her husband, Mr. Higgins, the gardener. Tony was there, too.

"Guess what? Guess what?" cried Henry.

"No guessing required," said Gilles, adjusting

his bow tie. "We all know while Mr. Heartwood is away, *I'm* in charge."

"As you keep reminding us. Mr. Heartwood obviously needed a break," said Mrs. Higgins. "His decision-making was clearly suffering." She frowned at Gilles's badge.

"I'm good at taking breaks. Right, Tilly?" piped Henry.

"There will be *no* time for breaks," the lizard said excitedly. "Spring is usually a steady season, but we will make it *bustle*! We will show Mr. Heartwood that he can take a rest without worry. We are the most wonderful hotel in Fernwood Forest. The *only* hotel in Fernwood Forest."

"No, we're not," burst Henry. "There's a new hotel in Fernwood!"

Gilles's tail twitched. "A new hotel? What do you mean?"

"Brumble came by," Mona hurried to explain.

"He said there's a new hotel opening up. A splashy one. He heard it from some birds."

Gilles's tail twitched again, so hard this time that it knocked a platter of seedcakes from Ms. Prickles's paws. The seedcakes fell to the floor with a crash.

Mrs. Higgins sighed at the mess. "Are you sure?" she asked Mona.

Mona shook her head. "Actually, no, ma'am. Brumble's never had the best memory."

But then Tony said, "I heard the same news from a passing messenger jay. All he told me was there's a new hotel still under construction, but supposedly it will change the flow of Fernwood. I thought he was trying to rile me up, but maybe not. Should someone go and find out more?"

"You mean *spy*?" said Henry eagerly, grabbing a seedcake from the floor.

"Henry . . ." scolded Tilly.

Gilles interrupted, "We are not spies! We have standards. Standards we must not lower but raise."

"Should we send a message to Mr. Heartwood, Gilles?" asked Mona.

Gilles shook his head. "Of course not. He's only just left. We must take care of this ourselves. Splashy, indeed! We'll show them splashy."

"What do you mean?"

"I've always told Mr. Heartwood that the spring needs more zing. The Heartwood Hop is too much like the Acorn Festival. It needs to be hoppier. . . ."

"I don't know . . . the Heartwood Hop sounds like fun," replied Mona.

"If you like hopping," said Henry, spitting out some seeds. "Hopping's for rabbits. *Games* are fun."

"Henry, hush!" said Tilly. "And what did I tell you? Chew before chatting!"

Gilles heard Henry, however, and his eyes gleamed. "Games! That's it! Not just games.

Competitions. Things the guests can really sink their paws into. A whole season of them. The snow-sculpting contest in the winter was a start, but there's so much more we could do! And to end it all, we'll make the biggest splash ever. A party to end all parties. A Spring Splash! We'll show them. We're the greatest hotel in Fernwood Forest, and that's a fact."

Mrs. Higgins shook her head. "I don't know."

But Gilles was turning a vibrant green. "Everyone, come on. Let's get in the splashy spirit. I need ideas for competitions."

"I've got some! I do, Mr. Manager, sir!" said Henry, bouncing off his seat.

Gilles glanced down at his badge and grinned. "Wonderful!" he cried.

Henry beamed. "Told you I can be helpful, Tilly."

"Caused us extra work, more like," grumped Tilly, but she rubbed his ears proudly.

Mona felt a knot form in her stomach. Usually *she* was the one with ideas.

As Henry hurried to help Gilles with his list, Tilly leaned over to Mona.

"I'm glad to see Henry so excited," said the squirrel. "This has all been a big change. At Hood's Home for Orphaned Animals, there were lots of kits like him. . . . Actually, that's what I was going to tell you, Mona. I need you to switch rooms with Henry. Please?"

The knot in Mona's stomach tightened. "Why?"

"Turns out Henry's not quite ready for his own. Even though Mrs. Higgins did clear out her sewing room specially."

"But . . ."

"There's only space in our room for two. Just think, no more noisy squirrel snoring!" Tilly teased.

"Your snoring's not that bad," replied Mona. "I mean, you *do* snore, but I was hoping to go through some of the old guest books with you tonight. I found them today, and I thought we could read them together, before bed. I'm hoping to find—"

Mona didn't even have a chance to finish before Tilly squeezed her paw. "Your parents! Maybe they wrote an entry! We'll find time to go through them," she said. "Even if we're in different rooms." Then she added, "As long as this whole Splash thing doesn't get too batty. Did I ever tell you about the time we had the bat birthday party here? Everything was upside down. *Actually* upside down!" she huffed.

Mona smiled and squeezed Tilly's paw back. But Mr. Heartwood gone? A new room? A Spring Splash? Mona couldn't help feeling that things were already turning upside down. It had nothing to do with bats, and everything to do with a certain little squirrel.

The Ruffled Robinsons

The Spring Splash began as suddenly as the buds burst open on the trees.

Mona had only just settled into her new room and hadn't started reading the guest books with Tilly yet when the Squirrels' Delivery Service arrived with flyers Gilles had ordered. Gilles proudly pinned the first one to the lobby mantel.

It seemed silly to advertise for the Splash without the events decided on, but Gilles wanted to get started at once. Mona sat at the front desk, on top of a stack of books, staring at the flyer.

The Heartwood Hotel presents the
Spring Splash!
An entire season of festivities
and competitions!

Grand Finale featuring
the Bluegrass Bandits

and the announcements of
winners!

Enjoy prizes,
Prickles's Petal Pastries,
and more!
Further details to be posted.

She had been told to check in guests while Gilles, Tilly, and Henry put up more flyers around the forest. They were, after all, much bigger than she was—even Henry—and could cover more ground. Mona was sure she and Tilly could easily have done the job, but there was no arguing with Gilles, especially now that he was the manager.

She tried not to let it bother her. Instead, she

organized the desk and made sure the room keys were hung neatly on the pegs behind it.

Realizing she had some free time, she was just about to fetch a guest book from upstairs to read when the front door swung open.

Mona peeked over the desk to find, flying into the hotel, two very ruffled robins and an egg. It was the bluest egg she'd ever seen, tucked in the fluffiest nest. The nest had a handle made of twigs on either side, which the robins were holding in their claws.

"Gently, dear! Gently!" cried the mother.

"I AM carrying it gently," said the father.

"Here, set it down, here. Like this."

Both of the robins landed carefully in front of the desk and peered in at the egg. "Oh no, the shell has a scratch," cried the

mother, who was wearing an apple-seed necklace. "Was it from a sharp twig?!"

"I knew the forest wasn't safe enough," said the father, who was wearing a red tie that exactly matched his chest feathers. He stroked the egg with his wing.

"That far part of Fernwood has too many dangers," said the mother. "We must protect Richard—"

"Roger," interrupted the father.

"Rosemary?" questioned the mother.

"I do like Rosemary," mused the father.

"Excuse me," said Mona.

The robins looked up at her.

"It's a mouse," said the mother. "Do you work here?"

"Yes. I'm Mona, a maid," she replied.

"But where is the badger?"

"Gilles, the lizard who would usually be here to greet you, is currently taking over for Mr.

Heartwood, who's away. But I can check you in."
Mona opened the check-in book.

"Mr. Heartwood isn't here?" The father straightened his tie and looked unsure. "I don't know. That was one of our reasons for coming here, to the Heartwood. A big badger to protect us and our egg. Our egg is very delicate, and there were far too many dangers in the forest for our liking. Foxes, weasels, eagles, hawks, owls . . ." He shuddered.

Mona shuddered, too. And so did the egg. It rocked in the nest.

"Oh, please, not so loud!" shushed the mother. "You know even mentioning them gives our dear egg nightmares."

"I can assure you the Heartwood is still the *safest* hotel in Fernwood Forest," said Mona. "'Sleep in safety, eat in earnest, and be happy at the Heartwood.' That's one of our mottos. We have *lots*."

She pointed to the signs that hung above the Heartwood fireplace: WE LIVE BY "PROTECT AND RESPECT," NOT BY "TOOTH AND CLAW" and GUESTS BIG OR SMALL, WE WELCOME ALL. There hung the flyer for the Splash, too, which reminded her.

"Not only are we the safest hotel, we're the splashiest," she added, sure that Gilles would want her to mention this. "Are you here for our big event?"

To Mona's surprise, however, the father shook his head.

"There's an event?" he asked.

"Yes. It's a special springtime festival for the Heartwood Hotel, competitions and . . . Well, we actually don't know all the events yet, but . . ."

"Oh dear," said the mother. "We were hoping for a quiet place for our egg, a safe place. We are first-time nesters, you see. The Robinsons. And we want nothing except the best for our dear Rupert."

"Rutabaga," coughed Mr. Robinson.

"Rutabaga? Definitely NOT Rutabaga." Mrs. Robinson shook her head.

"The Splash won't bother you," hurried Mona. "It's just games and fun activities for guests . . . like . . ." She stared at their egg. What could an egg do?

"Our egg would win any competition," said Mr. Robinson stoutly. "It's the sweetest."

"And the roundest," said Mrs. Robinson.

"And the cutest," finished Mr. Robinson. "No egg is cuter than ours. Let's stay. I'd love to see Rachel win her very first prize."

"Our egg, Ronald."

"Russell!"

Over the arguing of names, Mona checked them in and handed them a key. She watched as they headed up the stairs, holding the handles of the nest carefully between them in their beaks. Mona had offered to help, but they insisted on carrying it themselves.

Mona had never seen such particular parents. She wondered if they'd be disappointed when they found out the Splash had no contests for eggs. But it could. An idea hatched in her mind, a very splashy idea. The Cutest Egg Competition! *Gilles will be thrilled*, Mona thought with a smile.

The Cutest Egg Competition

"I'm thrilled!" said Gilles. Mona told him her idea the moment he came back from flyering the forest. Tilly and Henry had gone straight for food, but Gilles wanted to resume his front-desk position, even though he was tired. He perked up immediately when Mona shared her idea. "Why not? Let's encourage more birds to come with their eggs."

"Maybe they'll bring news about the new hotel, too," piped Mona, pleased.

"Indeed!" Gilles's color brightened. "I must get started on more flyers at once!"

This Week at the Heartwood Hotel's
Spring Splash:

~ 🥚 ~

The Cutest Egg Competition!
In the Courtyard
Nesting baskets provided

The flyers brought in a flock of flying guests, but no news of the new hotel. When the frogs arrived, they thought they might have heard a ripple of a rumor. They were more concerned, however, to find out whether all their eggs could be entered in the competition, or only one, since so many contestants had been signed up. Most families were booked in to stay all season, right to the Grand Finale.

"Nesting guests are the best!" declared Gilles, each time another family decided to stay.

Mona soon discovered they were also *a lot* of work. They needed the most room service, and since they never left their rooms, the only time to clean was during the competition, which meant she was stuck inside and didn't get to enjoy it.

"I tell you, speckles are the cutest!" chirped a swallow.

"One solid color looks SO much cuter!" replied Mrs. Robinson.

The birds' arguing drifted all the way up from the courtyard into the Robinsons' twig-floor suite, where Mona was cleaning. *Swish, swish, swish*, she swept with her dandelion broom, as quickly as she could. Maybe if she finished soon she could still watch some of the competition. If only Tilly were there to help. But since Mrs. Higgins wanted nothing to do with the Splash, Gilles had put Tilly, senior maid, in charge of event organization and judging, so Mona was alone.

 46

Well, almost alone . . .

"Mona, where's the chickadees' room? They forgot their egg's bonnet. The *frilly* one," Henry said with a grimace, bursting in.

"It's next door," said Mona. "Are you sure you—"

"I'm fetching things!" he proclaimed proudly. Then paused. "Which next door?"

"I better show you," said Mona, setting down her broom with a sigh.

The next time Henry came in, she was dusting the Robinsons' pictures. They were hanging from the roosting pegs, perched in the nest—the room was full of them!

Henry's mouth was full, too, of berry cake, which Mona knew was meant for the guests. You weren't supposed to eat guests' food. But Henry didn't seem to care. Or care about keeping his mouth closed either. "The froupm frgr . . ."

A spray of crumbs splattered Mona.

"Pardon?" asked Mona. "Henry, Tilly said chew before—"

Henry gulped. "The frogs forgot their favorite lily pad."

"It's in their bathtub," Mona replied. "And you really shouldn't eat . . ."

Too late, he was gone. All that was left were crumbs on the floor and a grump starting to sprout in Mona.

She was out on the balcony, refilling the Robinsons' birdbath, being careful not to splash (because there were even pictures out here), when Henry burst in again. This time, he waved a soft bark cloth.

"I have something for you, Mona. It's the Robinsons' egg shiner. They don't need it anymore. Where are you? Oh, you're outside. Here!" He held the cloth over his head, ready to throw it.

"Henry, not like that!" cried Mona.

"Catch!" Henry whipped the cloth to her.

It flew over her head and hit one of the Robinsons' pictures, perched on the side of the tub, knocking it into the water. *SPLASH!*

"Oh no!" cried Mona. She quickly fished for the picture, but it was already so soggy it fell apart in her paw.

Henry's face fell. "I . . . I didn't mean to. You should've caught it! I'm a *really* good thrower."

Mona felt the grump in her grow. She stormed inside, clutching what was left of the picture. "Look," she said, waving the soggy remains at Henry, "it's ruined. You should've brought the cloth to me instead of throwing it. You'd better go tell the Robinsons."

"But . . ."

Mona shook her head. "Now."

Henry left, and Mona put the picture in her dust basket, picked up her broom, and gave the room an extra-hard second sweeping. She knew the

Robinsons would be mad. Henry really shouldn't be helping out. He was too little. He wasn't a maid—he was a kit.

Suddenly Mona heard a shriek.

She rushed out to the Robinsons' balcony. Down below was a flurry of feathers, as the birds hopped around in a panic.

Oh no, thought Mona. *The Robinsons must REALLY not be happy. Maybe I shouldn't have made Henry go down there alone.* She hurried out of the room and down the stairs.

"Oomph!" As Mona was passing through the lobby, she collided with a very plump porcupine. Luckily, she wasn't poked by any of his quills.

"Oh, excuse me!" said Mona.

"No, no. Excuse *me,*" said the porcupine. His face was hidden by dark glasses and the extra-wide brim of a hat. A few of his quills, long and gray, stuck through the top of the hat. The porcupine

waved a piece of curled-
up birch bark. It was one
of the flyers. "I am
here for—"

"HENRY!"
Mrs. Robinson
shouted from the
garden.

Mona's paws itched to go outside, but she
couldn't be rude to a potential guest.

"You're here for our Splash? That's great," said
Mona. "If you would wait here, please, I will be
with you in a moment to check you in."

"Actually, I am Mr. Quillson from . . ."

Mona, however, was distracted. She listened for
more shrieking, but it had stopped, so she returned
her focus to the new guest.

". . . the hotel," finished the porcupine.

Did this porcupine just say he was from another

hotel? Could he be from the *new* hotel? But that didn't make sense. Now Mona wished she had been paying attention.

"I'm so sorry," she said, "but could you please say that again?"

The porcupine pointed to the bottom of the flyer: PRICKLES'S PETAL PASTRIES. "I would like a word with your cook, Petunia Prickles."

That's strange, thought Mona. Why would someone from another hotel want to speak with Ms. Prickles?

"I could send a message, if you'd like," she replied.

"I . . . um . . ." Mr. Quillson rolled up the flyer. "Hmmm. What I wish to say is best left to conversation."

"Should I book you in a room, then?" she asked.

"Yes. I suppose. Thank you."

As Mona quickly checked him in, she couldn't help but feel there was something slightly suspicious about Mr. Quillson. Especially when, as he left with his room key, Mona noticed that the porcupine had no luggage with him. No luggage whatsoever.

At last, Mona headed outside. The wind ruffled her fur and tugged at her apron.

In the courtyard, colorful eggs covered the mossy lawn, from tiny to large, spotted to stripy, in rows of pretty baskets. There was even a bucket of water with a cluster of frogs' eggs floating in it. But where was everyone?

Then Mona saw them, by one of the blackberry walls that framed the courtyard.

Henry was standing between the Robinsons, smiling sheepishly.

Around them, the birds—from wrens to sparrows to a giant pheasant—as well as a few frogs and some lizards, were raising cups of dew in a toast.

"To Henry!" said Mr. Robinson.

"To Henry!" agreed Mrs. Robinson. "He's an honorary egg."

Tilly, standing off to the side, saw Mona and waved her over with the notepad she used for judging. "What a disaster! Mona, you should've seen it."

"What happened?" Mona asked.

"It was the wind," explained Tilly. "Mrs. Robinson attached three leaf umbrellas to her basket to shield her egg, but that wasn't so smart because the wind caught them and blew the basket over. Her egg began to roll toward the black-berries with their huge thorns! Luckily, Henry was there. He saw and saved it before anything bad happened."

"Oh," said Mona.

"Best of all," continued Tilly, "the birds have

finally stopped arguing. They think Henry's the cutest, and a hero, besides."

Now Henry wasn't just good with ideas; he was a hero, too? But he had just ruined the Robinsons' picture. Did they know that? They must, because Mona heard Mrs. Robinson say, "And don't fret, Henry, over the picture. We want a new one drawn with you in it anyway."

Mona couldn't believe it!

Although she wished it wouldn't, she felt the grump part of her grow even bigger. She should be happy. Henry had saved the egg. But that's the thing about feelings. Sometimes you can't help them, as much as you might want to.

THE TINIEST TALENT SHOW

"Henry the hero" kept creeping into conversations over the next week. Henry was getting almost as much attention from guests and staff as from Tilly. But to Mona he was more of a headache than a hero—and became even more so when a firefly troupe, the Fernwood Flares, arrived for the next event, the Tiniest Talent Show.

It was Gilles's idea. "Now that the twig suites are filled, we need to fill all the six-legged ones, too," he had said. "We can have a talent show for the insects."

This week at the Heartwood Hotel's
Spring Splash:

~ ~ ~

卅 ☆ 卅

The Tiniest Talent Show
Under the full moon,
on the stargazing balcony
All tiny talents welcome!

Henry turned his broken acorn ball into a whistle to help the Flares practice their formations. The whistle made a loud, sharp screech and every time Henry blew it, Mona jumped. But the nesting birds didn't complain, so neither could she.

Luckily she was distracted by preparations for the event. Although there had been no more news of the new hotel, Gilles still wanted the Heartwood to be the best. And since Mona was a mouse, and the smallest of the staff, her paws were in high demand. Not only was she cleaning most of the bug suites (the millipede's was the worst—trying to sweep around all his shoes), she even got to help Ms. Prickles in the kitchen. Together, they made small sap strudels and mini muffins of wood rot for the family and friends of the little competitors. "Thank goodness for your help, dearie," said Ms. Prickles. "You have a knack with your paws, just like your mother."

That made Mona proud. She longed for a moment to look for an entry from her parents in the guest books, but she hardly had time to sleep, let alone read. It didn't help that Tilly hadn't even mentioned the books, despite her promise. Mona couldn't blame her: it really had become as batty as a bat's birthday party.

In fact, bats seemed to be the only guests who *hadn't* shown up. There were plenty of bugs, though. Practicing on the ceilings and rehearsing on the stairs. But not a single small guest had been stepped on—or eaten. Nor would they be, assured Gilles. Not at the most fabulous hotel in Fernwood.

Because of the fireflies' act, the Tiniest Talent Show was being held after sunset, on the stargazing balcony. The balcony was built on a giant branch, almost at the tip-top of the tree, and except for a cluster of lanterns that would light the stage, it was very dark. It was the perfect place for watching fireflies—and, of course, for gazing at stars.

The night of the show, the stars glimmered like silver leaves, and the forest wrapped itself around the hotel like a blanket of soft shadows. Mona was almost finished bringing up the tiny treats when she heard a loud noise. At first she thought it might be Henry's whistle. But it wasn't. It was a *CRASH!*

"Hello?" Mona called out.

From behind some of the balcony furniture that

had been stacked out of the way, against the tree trunk, emerged a large shape. It was the porcupine, Mr. Quillson.

"Excuse me," said Mona. "You shouldn't be back there."

The porcupine jumped. Mona could see his nose was flushed. "Oh—uh, I was just looking for . . ."

"Looking for what?" asked Mona. "Can I help you?" She stepped toward him.

"Perhaps later," he said, and hurried away.

How mysterious, thought Mona.

She peered back where the porcupine had come from. What had he been doing? He had knocked over a chair—and something else caught her eye.

There, carved into the tree, was a tiny heart. Guests weren't supposed to carve things into the tree. Except this looked old. The bark was curled around it, the wood itself weathered.

Could her dad have
carved it? He had carved
the heart on the hotel
door. But why? And
what was Mr. Quillson
doing looking at it? Mona
touched her paw lightly to
the carving.

There was a tug on her apron. "There you are.
May we have some muffins?"

Mona looked down from the heart to a group of
tiny ladybugs. "Of course," she said, and hurried
to fetch some.

Before long, the first contestants assembled to
the side of the stage that had been set up, and the
show began. In between serving treats to guests,
little and big, Mona watched in awe, all thoughts of
hearts and peculiar porcupines forgotten.

The ladybugs went first, dancing and singing:

"Hip hip hop, it's spring.
Hip hip hop, let's swing.
Bip bip bop, let's hop.
Bip bip bop, don't stop."

They were followed by the millipede, who did the forty-two-toed tap dance, and then a rabbit, who was definitely not tiny but had a tiny talent— painting a whole forest on a single seed. (Though it was hard for him to paint on the tiny stage!)

Three spit bugs showed off their spitting abilities, much to the dismay of some audience members who were sitting close to the stage, and a stinkbug demonstrated how he earned his nickname, "Super Stench," which he definitely deserved!

Just as Mona was fanning the air away, Tilly came rushing up to her.

"Mona, help!" Tilly gestured to the side of the stage with her notepad, where the final contestants, the Fernwood Flares, were waiting to go on. The bees were there, too.

"What's happening?" asked Mona.

"They're fighting. Really, the bees should be making honey, not criticizing guests. And I'm supposed to be judging!" Tilly threw up her paws. "I've had it up to here with all the arguing. And I *like* arguing. Mona, please. You're the best one to deal with this kind of thing."

"Don't worry. I'll calm them down," Mona said, and went to talk to Captain Ruby. The squadron of bees parted to let her through.

The captain was hovering in the air, facing a firefly called Florian, the leader of the troupe. On each of Florian's see-through black wings was a berry-stained *F*. When his wings were closed, they read *FF* for Fernwood Flares. Behind him were the rest of the fireflies.

"Our formations are the best," Florian was saying.

"Formations? I've seen your formations, and they will never be up to muster," said Captain Ruby.

"We Fernwood Flares have been doing light shows for years," replied Florian, with a flick of an antenna. "We invented the Bye-Bye-Blink."

"*BZZT!* Bye-bye, indeed!" muttered the captain.

"How can I expect one such as you to understand?" said the firefly. "True flying is about feeling. It's a fire that burns in your soul." He gazed up at the stars.

"Please . . ." Mona started.

But she didn't have a chance to say more, for the captain buzzed, "*Feeling?* The skies are for finely tuned squadrons, not *feelings*."

"Then why aren't YOU taking part in the talent show?"

"We were hired for our honey. But believe me—"

"Exactly! This talent show is not for you. It's for artists, those with a flame, a flare."

"How DARE you BE so belittling!"

"Please . . ." said Mona again. But the bee and firefly weren't listening!

TWEET! A whistle cut through the air. Henry's whistle! Mona hadn't noticed him standing nearby.

"AHA! Our signal!" cried Florian.

"But . . ." started Mona.

It didn't matter. The Fernwood Flares burst through the branches, into the sky. Everyone stopped what they were doing and looked up. Except the bees, who bitterly buzzed off.

Clustered into a tight ball, the fireflies made two spectacular flashes, both at the same time, then suddenly went dark. Mona thought the show was already over, but no. A second later the fireflies began to blink again, this time spiraling out in a pinwheel, until they looked like a giant sunflower in the sky. Then, in a burst, they soared off in a dozen different directions, like scores of shooting stars. The sky went dark again, this time for good. Only the real stars twinkled above.

"OOOO!" Everyone on the balcony gasped.

As the fireflies flew down to the stage, they were greeted with applause.

"Did you see that? Did you? I bet you everyone in Fernwood Forest did!" cried Henry, excited. His whistle dangled on a string around his neck. "They

did SUCH a good job! It was time for them to perform, and I stopped the fight. I helped, right?"

"You sure did," said Tilly, walking over.

"I guess . . ." said Mona, though she could see
Captain Ruby was hovering near the railing. The
captain did *not* look happy.

"The Flares were really good, weren't they?" said Henry, turning to his sister. "They're going to win, right?"

"HUSH, Henry, no one's supposed to know who wins until the finale," chided Tilly. "And how many of those pastries have you eaten?"

"Only . . . ten . . ." Henry looked guilty. "They're REALLY small."

"Humph. Come on, it's time to get you to bed."

As Tilly ushered Henry away, Mona turned to Captain Ruby, whose stinger was trembling with rage.

"That formation was full of holes," Captain Ruby buzzed. "It's unbelievable we weren't allowed to compete. I must speak with Tilly at once. . . ."

"Tilly is busy," said Mona. "But the Best Blossom Contest is next. Maybe you could help out some of the guests with that?"

"Flowers?" That seemed to make Captain

Ruby even madder. "Is THAT what you think we are good for?"

"I—I . . ." stammered Mona. "I'm sorry. I just thought . . ."

"It's simply that all bees know that the best blossoms grow in the Farmer's Garden at the far edge of Fernwood. That doesn't take skill. Formations take skill. You can never train enough. If I had started earlier . . ." The captain's buzz wobbled.

"What do you mean?" asked Mona.

"Before I was a captain and a queen, I was a princess. Our hive was destroyed by a bear. I was too small and unskilled to be of help. Never again, I vowed. Since then, I've never let my squadron set up a permanent base. It's safer that way."

"I'm so sorry to hear of your hive," said Mona gently. "I lost my home, too. The Heartwood's my home now, and I'd do anything for it. . . ."

The captain nodded. "You are quite the mouse.

I've heard of all your heroics. And I saw for myself your bravery with that bear—Brumble, was it?"

"Yes," said Mona, though dealing with Brumble didn't seem like such a brave act, since he was so friendly. "Not all bears are bad." Then she added, after a pause, "Maybe not all fireflies are either."

"BZZT!" Captain Ruby's tone changed. "I'll believe it when I see it. Right now, all I see are those fireflies exposing our flank." With that, Captain Ruby buzzed into the darkness, leaving Mona to wonder what exactly "exposing our flank" meant.

Was the captain saying that some kind of danger was coming?

She gazed into the night. The shadows felt sharper than soft now, and Mona couldn't help but shiver.

THE BEST BLOSSOM CONTEST

The next few weeks were so busy, Mona forgot all about Captain Ruby's warning. Most of the birds' eggs had hatched, and every morning (and much of the day, too) was a rush of room service bringing meal trays to their suites.

Actually, Mona didn't mind. She liked seeing the baby birds, even if they were more wrinkly than cute! Still, it often meant she missed her own breakfast—and there was definitely no time for reading guest books.

Today at the Heartwood Hotel's

Spring Splash:

~ ✳ ~

The Best Blossom Contest

Bring blossoms to bedeck a balcony

The final event before the

FINALE!

So Mona was surprised the morning of the Best Blossom Contest to see Tilly in the hall, with a guest book in her paws. Mona felt a surge of happiness.

"You remembered!"

Tilly frowned. "Oh, this one is blank. Gilles wanted me to fetch it. There's a meeting in the lobby. Our other one was full already. It's some kind of record. I haven't forgotten about the guest books, really. It's just . . ."

"I know," said Mona, frowning now, too.

"Maybe this will help?" said Tilly, slipping her

a seedcake from her apron pocket as they headed upstairs.

It wasn't the same as reading the guest books, but the seedcake *was* good to munch on, and she gave Tilly a smile.

When they got to the lobby, the other staff were already there. Gilles was standing in front of the fireplace, adjusting his bow tie and looking pleased with himself. Every day, he seemed to be turning a brighter shade of green. Today he was as green as a grasshopper and just as jumpy.

"Aha, there you are!" Gilles flicked his tongue. "Put the book on the front desk, Tilly, and we can begin."

"What's going on?" Mona asked.

"Another contest!" said Henry.

Another contest? Mona and Tilly rolled their eyes at each other.

"Gilles is nuts," whispered Tilly. "Not the tasty kind. The crazy kind."

"The finale is tomorrow," said Mona.

"I know!"

Clearly the rest of the staff felt the same.

"Gilles, I must return to the garden," said Mr. Higgins. "I'm not finished setting up the stage."

"And I need to go over the schedule for tomorrow," added Tilly.

"If you must do something, Gilles, why not decorate?" suggested Mrs. Higgins.

"Yes, yes! That's EXACTLY what I was thinking!" said Gilles. "We have a full hotel. The band has practiced—the famous Bluegrass Bandits. What a booking! And the fireflies are primed. What talent! I was so impressed with their performance, I've hired them to perform tomorrow night. Most guests are out now finding blossoms, and I thought: Why should the guests have all the fun? Why not make it a competition for the staff, too?

Surely the other hotel would never let their staff participate in a competition. But the Heartwood treats everyone the best. It will get us even more energized and in the mood for the grand finale. And we can use the blossoms to *decorate*. I want to *cover* the entire tree."

"So if one of us wins, *we* get the prize?" asked Maggie, one of the laundry rabbits.

"Yes, yes. Whoever finds the best blossom—guest or staff—wins a free stay in the penthouse suite. Once the Splash is over, of course. You can invite anyone you choose to stay with you."

Everyone was instantly excited. That *was* a good prize. Henry began jumping up and down. "Can I play, too? Can I?"

"You're not staff, Henry," said Tilly. "And you're not really a guest either. I'm not sure. I AM sure that I can't. Humph. It's not fair. I wish I could look, but I have to be the judge."

"Come on, Tilly. Please." Henry tugged on

Tilly's apron. "I'm good at smelling! I can find the best blossom!"

The best blossom . . .

Mona remembered what the bees had told her. The best blossoms were in the Farmer's Garden. She knew where that was. Long ago, before coming to the Heartwood, Mona had stayed in the barn at the edge of the forest. It was far away, but she could get there. She was "quite the mouse," after all. Which everyone seemed to have forgotten. But if she won the best blossom . . .

"I'm going to participate," said Mona. "I—"

"Great!" said Tilly. "I was hoping you'd take him."

Mona didn't mean that, but now it was too late.

"Stick close to Mona, okay?" Tilly told Henry. "Don't go too far. And make sure you're helpful." She rubbed between his ears. "Thanks so much, Mona."

Mona looked over at Henry, who was jumping

up and down extra enthusiastically. It seemed she didn't have any choice.

Pushing a little luggage cart to carry back the blossom, Mona headed off into the forest, Henry by her side.

Spring had not only brought Fernwood Forest to life, but it had brought out many of the animals who lived there. Through some branches, in a hollow, Mona could see a little deer taking its wobbly

first steps, its mama proudly looking on. A vole was vigorously sweeping dust from his tree-root doorway, and three gopher pups were skipping with a rope of braided grass. Henry looked at them longingly.

"Come on," said Mona. "We have flowers to fetch."

Henry perked up and ran ahead. "I found some!" he said.

A few white daisies and blue forget-me-nots dotted the mossy trail along the bank of the stream. Mona shook her head.

"There are better flowers farther on," she said. Mona knew if they followed the stream, it would lead them all the way to the Farmer's Garden.

So they continued walking beside the warbling water. Henry began to sing, too:

"Hip hip hop, it's spring.
Hip hip hop, let's swing.

Bip bip bop, let's hop.
Bip bip bop, don't stop."

His voice was loud and off-key. Even so, Mona caught herself humming along. After a while, Henry stopped singing and started asking questions.

"Mona, did you really live in the forest all by yourself before you lived at the Heartwood?"

Mona nodded, pushing the luggage cart. "Yes. A barn for a while and an old tree stump, too."

"Was it lonely?"

Sometimes, but she didn't want to admit this to Henry. "It can be nice to be alone and *quiet*."

Henry didn't take the hint. "I could never live all by myself. I'd be too . . ." Henry stopped and sniffed. His tail twitched. "Do you smell that?"

Mona sniffed, too. All she could smell were the moss and the maple trees, and she told him so.

"No. Something else. I'm not sure what . . . but—" He shivered. "I don't like it."

"It's just your imagination." Mona pushed the cart over a root. The wheel stuck.

"Here, I can help," said Henry. "I'm bigger than you. I mean, I know I'm *littler* but I'm still *bigger.*" He grabbed the cart away from Mona and shoved. *POP!* The wheel burst free from the roots. Henry lost his grip and the cart raced ahead of them, down the trail. *CRASH!* It hit a rock and toppled over.

"Henry!" cried Mona. "Now look what you've done. Just because I'm a mouse doesn't mean I can't do it."

Henry gulped. "I was just trying to help."

"Never mind . . ." Mona sighed. "Let's go."

Henry looked at the cart in the distance and shook his head.

"Nuh-uh, Mona. I smell something *bad.*"

"You stay here, then. This is the way to the best blossom. I'll come get you after."

Henry's eyes went wide.

"Look," said Mona, "you don't have a choice.

I'm not going back, so you can't either. There's no one to take you."

But as it turned out, there was.

As though it was meant to be, Mona heard the voices of Maggie and Maurice through the trees.

"Clover flowers! Yum!" said Maurice.

"No, Maurice, don't EAT them," said his sister. "We'll *never* win the prize if you *eat* our entries. I told you, we can have lunch once we get back to the Heartwood." Maggie and Maurice were heading back to the hotel!

"There," Mona said to Henry, "problem solved. You can go with them."

"Are you *sure?*" Henry replied. But he sniffed again and shivered.

"I'm sure," said Mona. If Henry went back, she could find a blossom all by herself. "And besides, you don't want to miss lunch. I'll catch up with you later."

That did it. Henry nodded and scurried toward

the voices. His red tail was the last thing to disappear through the bushes. It looked surprisingly small and droopy.

It's better like this, Mona told herself. Tilly wouldn't be mad at her for leaving him with Maggie and Maurice. Henry was safe with them—safer than heading out so far into the forest anyway.

With Henry gone, Mona scrambled down the trail to the cart. It took all her strength and several tries to get it back on its wheels. But at last she managed it and was on her way again.

Time passed slowly, and the forest was eerily quiet without Henry's chatter.

It's just because of the weather, thought Mona. Sun wasn't shining through the canopy anymore. Gray sky peeked between the green leaves. Was it going to rain? Wind blew through, picking up petals and fluff, and even some Splash flyers. They really *had* been posted everywhere.

One swooped by Mona, like a spooky wing.

Others joined it, circling her head like birds of prey. She could only read a few words: *competitions . . . finale . . . Prickles.*

Mona's tail began to tremble, and the fur on her neck stood up.

Should she head back to Henry and the rabbits? To the Heartwood? But then she thought of returning with the best blossom.

Go on, she told herself, pushing her cart extra fast. *There's no one else here. It's only your imagination.*

It wasn't, though, because a moment later she heard a low voice.

SKIM THE SNAIL

"Salutations!"

Mona froze.

"Salutations!" came the voice again.

Mona looked around frantically, but she couldn't see anyone *anywhere*.

"Hello?" she whispered.

"Under here," came the voice.

Mona pulled the luggage cart back, cautiously, to reveal right in front of it . . .

A snail! Mona breathed a sigh of relief. Henry was wrong. A snail was nothing to be scared of.

The snail's feelers were curled upward like a

moving mustache, and he was wearing large round glasses. How they were perched on his eye stalks, Mona wasn't sure. Perhaps they were stuck on with slime? His shell was a swirl of reds, like a tiny rosy apple. He was, Mona realized, an apple snail. Usually they lived in water, but they traveled on land, too. She had met a few on her adventures in the woods, before coming to the Heartwood. Slung over this snail's shell was the strap of a suitcase, which was made from another shell—an itty-bitty clam one.

The snail looked up at Mona and blinked. His eyes were magnified by the lenses of his glasses. "Perhaps you can help. I'm looking for my hotel. My brother booked me there as a birthday gift."

"You must be one of our guests," said Mona. "I'm one of the maids. My name is Mona."

"How fortuitous," said the snail. "Am I going the right way? I really should have brought a map."

"Yes, you are," said Mona.

"Thank goodness. It IS a good thing I ran into you. Or, shall I say, you ran into me. No need to look dismayed. I should have spoken up. I was trying to remember the directions. I must have read them too quickly. I'm a fast reader—a speed-reading champion, in fact—and sometimes that can get me into trouble because I skip over things."

"Speed-reading champion?" Mona asked.

"Yes. My name is Skim," the snail said, blinking behind his glasses. "Now, this convergence was a pleasure, but I must keep going."

Mona watched as the snail began to slowly inch his way forward to the Heartwood. *Very* slowly.

It would take him at least a day *and* a night to reach the Heartwood at the rate he was traveling.

As much as she wanted to find the best blossom and win the contest, she couldn't leave a guest alone in the forest, so far away from the Heartwood. Mr. Heartwood would never do that. Suddenly, with an ache, Mona missed the big badger.

"I can take you there, if you'd like," she said to the snail.

"Would you?" The snail perked up. "I really could use a quiescence."

"Excuse me?"

"A rest," the snail explained. "It has been a long journey. I may be a speed-reading champion, but in all other matters, I am extremely slow."

Indeed by the time he'd inched his way onto the luggage cart, the rain had started to fall, a few drops slipping through the canopy, and Skim was happy about it. The pitter-patter of the rain mixed with his chattering as Mona rolled him back to the hotel.

They could hear the hubbub before the Heartwood came into sight. It had taken them a long time to get back, even with Skim riding the cart. But Mona didn't realize quite how long she'd been gone until she saw the hotel.

White daisies, blue violets, yellow buttercups, chocolate lilies, blue forget-me-nots, and pink-and-white trilliums, all braided together in chains, were being looped through the balcony railings by the guests and staff, who were singing and shouting as they worked. Some were even preening their feathers and fur in the spring shower. Others were tucking ferns and grasses into the bark of the tree. Mona could smell the sweetgrass and the wild oats. And the skunk cabbage! Petals floated and filled the pool that the stream created between two roots.

The hotel was almost unrecognizable. It didn't even look like a tree! It looked . . .

"*Grandiferous!*" declared Skim.

"What does that mean?" asked Mona.

"I made it up," said Skim. "Sometimes the best words burst from you, in the heart of the moment."

"Oh," said Mona.

"Though I must say, it isn't what I expected."

It wasn't what Mona expected either. Was it really grandiferous? She wasn't sure. "Come on," she said to Skim. "I can check you in."

The inside of the Heartwood was just as colorful and chaotic as the outside. If at the beginning of spring, the hotel had been buzzing with energy, now it was bursting. Guests were coming and going down the stairs—hatchlings who couldn't fly yet were even sliding down the rail. Crickets chirped from the ceiling of the lobby. Chipmunks were eating nuts in the empty fireplace. The beautiful new lobby rug was being scrubbed by a family of pigs.

"Mud is for sunscreen, not for rugs," the mama pig was saying to her piglets. Tilly had said the pigs were tidy, but this was ridiculous. They wouldn't even let Mona wipe her feet on it.

Maggie and Maurice didn't seem to care that guests were cleaning. They were draping daisy chains above the fireplace mantel, hiding the Heartwood motto. Mr. Heartwood would never allow that. Near them, Mona could see the porcupine, Mr. Quillson, a cluster of daisy chains in his paw. But instead of handing them to the rabbits to arrange, he was plucking petals from one of the flowers and muttering to himself. Extra strange!

"Mona, you're back!" said Maggie. "Where's your flower?"

Of course, she hadn't had a chance to find one.

"You should see what Henry found," added Maurice.

Sure enough, there was Henry. Mona was relieved to see him—until she noticed the giant blossom he was holding. The pink flower was shaped like a heart. It was just the sort of flower she would have liked to find.

"It's a heart flower!" said Henry. "You know, like the Heartwood! Want to help me put it up?"

"I have a guest to check in," said Mona, a bit of grump creeping into her voice, and wheeled the cart away from Henry toward the front desk.

But when she checked the ledger, there was no record of Skim, or any snails, for that matter.

"Let me talk to Gilles," said Mona. "He's our manager. One moment."

She found Gilles in Mr. Heartwood's office, which was at the back of the front desk. The door was slightly open. Gilles looked small in Mr. Heartwood's big twig chair. He was arguing with Mrs. Higgins.

"This is ridiculous, Gilles! We have a secret

door for a reason, to make our hotel hard to find. But *everyone* can find the hotel now."

"Exactly!" said Gilles. "We want EVERYONE to come here."

"No, we don't!" huffed Mrs. Higgins. "We have no room."

"Um . . ." started Mona, reluctant to interrupt.

"Mona, there you are!" said Mrs. Higgins. "More of the hatchlings have been born. Their rooms need cleaning. The shells must be properly recycled—taken to the garden for composting—unless of course the parents wish to keep pieces for mementos."

"But Gilles sent us to get blossoms," said Mona.

Mrs. Higgins huffed again.

"I did, but that was ages ago. Everyone came back with plenty," said Gilles. "Now, please, if we are to manage this Splash, I must have you here. Why, it's a fully booked hotel. Every room is occupied."

95

"We're fully booked? But we have a guest here now, waiting for a room," said Mona.

Gilles's tongue flicked out, then in. "We do?"

"He said he has a reservation."

"See? Our standards are slipping!" tsked Mrs. Higgins. "If you would spend more time at the desk . . ."

"We'll find him a room, we must!"

"But how?" asked Mona. "You just said there were none left."

"I did. There aren't." Gilles got up and began poring over the large map of the hotel hanging on the wall. "I just booked a family of rabbits into the last ones. Fourteen kits. I gave them three rooms. They *are* related to the Duchess." He was so green now, he practically glowed.

"This is a snail. He wouldn't need a big room. Maybe something in the bug suites?" piped Mona.

Gilles shook his head, tapping the map with

his tail, harder and harder each time. "Booked, booked, booked!"

If Gilles felt dreadful, Mona felt worse, as she peered back through the office door. Skim had inched himself over to the guest book on the front desk and seemed to be reading it.

Suddenly Mona had an idea. "Gilles, there IS one room left." She pointed to the map.

"But that's the storage room. It's filled with books," said Mrs. Higgins. "It will NEVER do."

"Actually," said Mona, "I think for this guest, it will be just right."

And it was. Despite the mix-up, Skim was ecstatic, which he explained to Mona meant "very happy indeed."

Once Mona had cleaned the suite, the snail settled in with a tub of water, a dandelion-leaf sandwich, and a big stack of books. "If there is anything I can do for you, Miss Mouse," he said, "I would be happy to. You have taken great care of me."

"Actually," said Mona hesitantly, another idea popping into her head, "if you are going to read the guest books anyway, could you look for an entry for me, please . . . by mice? My parents, Madeline and Timothy, stayed here long ago. I don't know their last names. They were lost in a storm when I was a baby. I've been trying to read the books myself, to see if they wrote an entry, but I haven't had a chance. I'm not a fast reader like you."

"Of course," said Skim. "It's but a night's wordswork."

Mona smiled. Wordswork? It was another one of Skim's made-up words. But it sounded perfect.

10

A Tiff with Tilly

☆ TONIGHT! ☆

GRAND FINALE

☆ OF THE ☆

SPRING SPLASH!

*B*ANG! *BAM! BOOM!*

The sounds that woke up Mona the next morning were anything but perfect. Not one, but two
bands were battling down the hallway. They were
so loud the noise drifted all the way to Mona's
room. She got out of bed, tied her apron on with a

quick knot, and peeked out her door. All along the hallway other staff were doing the same.

Outside Mrs. Higgins's office, three raccoons were yelling at three frogs. Mrs. Higgins and Gilles were there, still wearing their nightcaps and looking frazzled.

BANG! One of the frogs hit his drum. "We are always hired for the Heartwood Hop!"

TWANG! One of the raccoons plucked his banjo. "But it's NOT the hop. It's the Splash. And *we* were hired."

"Didn't you cancel the Hoppers?" Mrs. Higgins said to Gilles.

"I . . . ah . . . I . . ." For once Gilles seemed at a loss for words. But then he found some. "I . . . decided to book you both." The bands didn't look happy about this, but at least they stopped their noise.

Mona was glad that fighting was over. In the kitchen, however, she was greeted by another argument.

Captain Ruby had found out that the Flares had been asked to perform that night and was none too pleased.

"Can't we book them, too?" Mona asked Gilles when he came in. "Like you did with the bands?"

"The bees are already booked—to make honey," he replied.

"Fine," said the captain. "Since we are not being given a chance to display our fine-tuned formations, we shall depart for good. First thing tomorrow. THOSE Flares are always the only ones who get to shine." The squadron buzzed away.

"Oh dear," cried Ms. Prickles. "Now look what's happened." Smoke filled the kitchen. Mona hurried to help.

"I've never burned anything before, not in all my years," she moaned.

"Never?" asked Mona.

She paused. "I guess there was that one time, when I was young and let my heart distract my head. . . ."

Mona wondered what Ms. Prickles meant and hoped she would say more. But she didn't. Instead, the porcupine composed herself and continued,

"It's okay, dearie. I'll just save them for Henry. He won't mind. He has an even bigger appetite than his sister."

Henry again? Now he was the best eater, too? This was getting ridiculous!

By the afternoon, things had calmed down considerably, as almost everyone was busy brushing their fur and fluffing their feathers to get ready for the big party.

Tilly, though, was running around, frantically assigning roles to the staff for later. Gilles was master of ceremonies. Ms. Prickles was going to serve her petal pastries. Even Tony, the security woodpecker, had a task: as well as patrol, he had to relight any lanterns that might blow out.

What will I get to do? wondered Mona. *Something important*, she decided. Tilly still hadn't told her, only asked her to place the lanterns around the edge of the stage in the courtyard. It was supposed to be a dark night with only a whisker of a moon, and lanterns were needed.

Mona was setting them up now. They were made of seed shells, with candles inside, and would brightly light the stage and cast a soft glow over the courtyard, where guests would sit and eat. Mona had just placed the last lantern, wondering what her special task would be, when she heard something. Muttering from in the forest.

She tiptoed to the back of the stage. There, she could just make out a spiny silhouette. Mr. Quillson. He was skulking in the shadows and talking to himself. This wasn't just mysterious—this was suspiciously sneaky! He was up to something. But what?

She remembered what he had said when she first met him, about being from another hotel. Was he from *the* hotel? The splashy one? Maybe he was here trying to steal the Heartwood's secrets. She'd been too distracted by the Splash to think of it before. But it made sense.

With everyone outside, it would be a perfect chance for him to sneak around. He'd have the whole Heartwood to himself.

I have to watch out for him. That should be my task for tonight, thought Mona.

That was an important job. Who better to do it than her? She would tell Tilly at once.

But Tilly had other plans for her.

Mona found Tilly hurrying up the stairs. The squirrel was all dressed up. She wasn't wearing her apron. Instead, a stylish spiderweb scarf was wrapped around her neck. Her tail wasn't bushy or bristly either. It was curled in neat ringlets. There was even a bow tied between her ears.

Mona was still wearing her apron. The heart on

it was smudged with dirt. She wished she could go change, too. If they were still sharing a room, they could have gotten ready together.

"Mona, there you are. Everything is ready, but there is something important I need you to do," said her friend.

"Watch Mr. Quillson?"

"Mr. Quillson? No. I need you to watch Henry."

Mona's whiskers stiffened.

"You looked after him yesterday," continued Tilly. "He really liked it."

He liked it? Mona couldn't believe it. She'd sent him back with Maggie and Maurice.

Tilly went on, "There's so much to do tonight. I won't be able to keep a proper eye on him. It would be great if you made sure he eats something healthy. Not just the petal pastries. He should go to bed right after the Flares do their fireworks. I promised him he could use his whistle to signal them to start. He's really excited about that."

Tilly straightened the bow between her ears.

"No," said Mona quietly.

"Thanks, Mona. I knew I could count on you," said Tilly, turning to head outside to the courtyard.

"No," Mona said, louder this time.

"What?" said Tilly, spinning around.

"No, Tilly," said Mona, quickly, before she lost her courage. "I'm not a squirrel-sitter. I'm a maid."

"But Henry—"

Right then, the grump in Mona, the one that had been growing all season, burst out of her. "Henry, Henry, Henry! It's always about him."

"He's my brother, Mona," said Tilly. "He's family!" Tilly's cry caused a few rabbit guests, who were walking past, to hop extra high. Tilly lowered her voice, but continued in a rush, "Just because he's a star here doesn't mean you have to be so mean. I can't believe that I'd ever say this, but you're out-grumping even me!"

Maybe it was true. But Mona didn't care. "Star?!

He's not a star, he's a kit. He doesn't belong here. Nothing is the same. Not you, not us, not even the Heartwood. And it's all because of Henry. He's YOUR brother. You're the one who should be looking after him, not me. I'm a maid. I've got my own jobs to do."

"Then you'd better find one of those jobs to do tonight!"

"I will! Here." Mona gestured toward the Heartwood lobby. "Someone needs to stay inside and look after the Heartwood. I don't care if I don't see you, or Henry, or . . ."

But at that very moment, she did see Henry.

He was right in front of her, peeking around the ballroom doorway. He looked crestfallen. How much had he heard? Before she could say anything, he disappeared. Suddenly it felt like Mona had swallowed a rock.

Tilly hadn't seen him.

"FINE!" the squirrel cried. And with that, Tilly turned her back on Mona and huffed down the hall.

For a moment, Mona stood there, unsure what to do. Should she go after Henry? No. She'd only told the truth. Henry would find Tilly. They had each other. She didn't need them.

Mona stormed down the hall, into the lobby, away from Tilly, away from the back door that led out to the courtyard and to the party.

Away from everyone.

MONA'S MOMENT

Not everyone. There was still one guest left in the Heartwood. Caught up in her anger, Mona almost tripped over Skim the snail.

He was slowly inching down the hall. His glasses were polished so they shone. His shell, too. It looked like it was coated with a special glittery slime.

"Ah, Mona," said Skim. "I hoped to encounter you!"

Mona took a deep breath to calm herself down.

"I read the guest books last night," the snail continued.

"ALL of them?" Mona couldn't believe it.

"I'm not a speed-reading champion for nothing." Skim grinned.

"And . . . ?" This was just what she needed. Mona's heart hummed with hope. At last she'd find out what her parents had written.

"As I said, I read all the guest books. Did you know that the famous poet Tennyson the turtle stayed here?"

"And . . ." prompted Mona.

"And the cherished chipmunk author Louisa May Acorn?"

"And my parents," said Mona.

"Yes, your parents," replied the snail. "In regard to them, I am afraid there were no entries from mice named Madeline or Timothy."

"Are you sure?"

"Positively."

Immediately Mona's heart sank.

Skim blinked several times. "Perhaps . . ." he started.

"Thank you," Mona managed to choke out. She didn't need to hear more. She knew what "positively" meant. She *knew* she shouldn't have expected there to be an entry from her parents, but she *had* so wished there was. And, of course, Skim had to tell her the bad news now. What was the saying? Bad nuts always came in threes. Well, that was two.

Mona added a polite "Enjoy the party," and made her way past the snail to the lobby, which was empty now. Everyone was out-side. She didn't even bother to get some books to sit on. She plunked down behind the front desk with an angry thump and disappeared from view.

Why did she and Tilly *always* have to fight? This time felt worse than ever. And it was all because of Henry.

Laughter carried in from outside as the grand

celebration began. Someone must have left the back door open. The party was so loud. Even in the lobby. Especially since the Bluegrass Bandits *and* the Hippity Hoppers were playing at the same time. The two bands were still competing.

Mona *could* shut the door, but there was a part of her that wanted to listen. Even though it made her unhappier. When you are mad, sometimes it feels like the whole world is having fun, except for you. And in Mona's case, it really seemed like it was.

Right when she thought she couldn't stand it a second longer, Gilles shouted, "STOP!" and the music paused.

"Thank you all for coming to the Splash!" said Gilles enthusiastically. "Isn't this the biggest? The fanciest? The SPLASHIEST? Isn't the Heartwood the best hotel in all of Fernwood Forest?!"

The audience applauded in agreement.

"Now, it's time for what you've all been waiting for—our grand-prize announcements. First, the results of the Cutest Egg Competition. The winner will receive this lovely eggshell mosaic."

The audience cheeped and cheered.

"And . . . the prize goes to the Robinsons' egg, Riley . . ." came Gilles's shout.

"Rudy . . . !"

"Rona . . . !"

"Yes, yes," said Gilles. "Here you go! Now, aren't you both glad you stayed for the Heartwood's MARVELOUS Splash?"

"We are!" chirped Mr. Robinson.

"Careful, dear," chided Mrs. Robinson.

There was a pause, and Mona figured they were carrying their egg off the stage. She could hear some birds still arguing: "They only won because *their* egg hasn't hatched yet."

Gilles continued, "Next we present the award for the Tiniest Talent Show, a teeny-tiny trophy. The winner? No surprises here . . . the Fernwood Flares!"

The audience began to clap again, but Gilles said, "Hold your applause, though. The Flares will be collecting their prize later. They are busy warming up inside. They have a fantastic show planned for us tonight. And," the lizard added, "the final prize! May I have a drumroll, please!"

He got not one but two. And they grew louder and louder.

"OKAY! Thank you, Bandits and Hoppers. That's enough. The prize for the Best Blossom, a free stay in the penthouse suite, goes to . . . Henry the squirrel."

The audience exploded with cheers.

Henry had won! Mona couldn't believe it.

"Henry?" came Gilles's voice again, over the clapping. Mona imagined the little squirrel making his way to the stage, his tail growing bigger and bigger, fluffier and fluffier. Tilly would be looking on proudly.

Could this night get any worse?

Yes, it could. As if in answer to her question, Mona heard a shriek. A shriek that by now she recognized well.

The Robinsons. *What had happened to their egg this time?*

But it was more than the Robinsons' egg.

RAT-A-TAT! RAT-A-TAT-A-TAT! Tony was sounding the alarm!

What was going on?

Mona *knew* it. She *knew* there was going to be trouble. She hadn't seen hide nor quill of Mr. Quillson inside the hotel. He must be outside. He was trying to ruin the Splash. Had he punctured some of the lanterns? Tipped over the food table? Somehow made the stage collapse?

Or maybe it was Henry. Maybe one of his antics hadn't ended well. At last Tilly would see the truth, how it was all his fault. He wouldn't be able to save the day this time. *But I will,* thought Mona.

She slid down from the chair and ran to the back door, flinging it fully open.

But it wasn't Mr. Quillson. Or Henry. Or even the Robinsons.

It was something far, far worse.

DARKNESS DESCENDS

*O*WLS!

Four of them, gliding down from the night sky to attack. They were huge and gray, with feathered horns and eyes that blazed like forest fires. Not screech owls, or burrowing owls, or snowy owls. These were great horned owls, the wolves of the sky. But instead of howling or growling—or even hooting—they were spine-chillingly silent. Their sharp talons were extended and spread so wide they could pluck up a porcupine. . . .

SWOOP! One was headed right for Ms. Prickles! Mr.

Quillson threw himself at her, and together they tumbled, just in time, underneath the stage.

"HIDE! HIDE! HIDE!" cried Gilles, pushing other animals under the stage, too. It was the only safe place in the courtyard.

SWOOP! Another owl flew down, its talons almost catching Gilles's tail before the lizard himself dove to safety.

SWOOP! This time an owl was headed right for Mona. She froze in the doorway.

"GO BACK, MONA! GO!" came a high-pitched shout. Was it Tilly?

Mona didn't know, couldn't see, couldn't breathe, as the owl, his beak bigger than her head, plunged toward her. His talons were reaching and his eyes were fixed on her. At least, one eye was.

The other eye was a mass of scars. The owl's talons grazed Mona's apron, tearing the little heart from it.

No! thought Mona. *Tilly made that for me.* In her moment of anger, her paws unfroze. She tumbled backward through the doorway and slammed the door shut, just in time, blocking the owl from sight.

As soon as she caught her breath, she rushed to the ballroom to peer out the window for a view of the back of the hotel.

Many of the lanterns had been smashed, but enough light remained for Mona to see the chaos in the courtyard.

Tables and chairs had been knocked over and petal pastries littered the lawn. All that was left on the stage were the instruments and sheet music in shreds. The animals, guests and staff alike, were huddled under the stage. Gilles, Ms. Prickles, and Mr. Quillson. Maggie and Maurice. Mr. and Mrs. Higgins. The Robinsons, clutching their egg. And the other birds and their chicks and hatchlings, eyes wide and unblinking, beaks open in horror.

But where was Tilly? Mona squinted and could just make out her friend, her tail no longer curled neatly but a tangle of red. Tilly was crying. Where was Henry? He wasn't beside Tilly.

Mona scoured the animals, searching, only to notice that all the guests and staff—the ones she could see anyway, were looking up.

A deep shiver ran down her spine, right to the tip of her tail.

Mona didn't need the other animals' gazes to know that the owls were there, roosting on the Heartwood's branches. She could feel it in her

whiskers, and she could hear them, too—chilling hoots, the only music now at the Splash.

The Splash! That's what had caused this. Mona remembered the flyers far out in the forest, floating free for any owl to see, the arguing and shrieks at the Cutest Egg Competition, the loud applause and bright lights of the Tiniest Talent Show, and the blossoms, like beacons, drawing attention, good and bad, to the tree.

"Sleep in safety, eat in earnest, and be happy at the Heartwood." That was one of Mr. Heartwood's mottos. But they had all forgotten it. No one was safe or happy now. Mr. Heartwood would *never* have been so careless.

But Mr. Heartwood wasn't there. She was all alone. It was up to her to save the hotel. With the wolves, and in the snow, she always had others' help.

If only there was someone. Tilly, or Ms. Prickles, or even Gilles. Without anyone there— what would she do? Never had Mona felt so scared.

CRACK! An owl swooped down and crushed a lantern with its talons, putting out the light. *CRACK! CRACK! CRACK!* Suddenly all was dark. A chorus of panicked voices cried for help.

Mona stumbled back across the room, in a panic now herself. Her heel struck something—a root?—and she fell down and started to cry.

Hopeless, helpless sobs.

And then she heard crying that wasn't her own. It was faint and seemed to be coming from below her, as though from the root itself.

She knew the tree was alive, but it couldn't cry. She wiped her nose and listened very closely. Yes, there was definitely crying.

Mona pressed her ear against the root. The sound was much louder. She felt around until she came to a surprise: a small hollow, a handle—a door!

Better Together

Mona tugged the handle, but had to use both paws before the trapdoor creaked open. There was a light from below, a lantern flickering halfway down a small staircase.

"Hello?" she whispered. No one answered.

The crying had stopped. She took a few tentative steps down the stairs and peered into the shadows. At the bottom was a cramped space, and—were those silhouettes she saw? Was this a secret tunnel from the courtyard? Maybe the guests and staff had rescued themselves!

"Hello!" Mona called again, eagerly, hurrying

down the last steps, only to be disappointed. They were only costumes, hanging from hooks on the walls. There was Mr. Heartwood's red cap and bag from when he dressed up as St. Slumber, and some other outfits, too. There was even a wedding dress that was full of holes, as though it had been munched by a moth or worn by a porcupine.

This must be a secret changing room, thought Mona.

Or maybe not-so-secret. One of the costumes moved. There *was* somebody there.

"Hello?" Mona said again.

Still no one answered. But the costume shifted and revealed a red tail she would recognize anywhere.

"Henry?" said Mona. Mona pushed the costume aside, and there was the little squirrel, sniffling and rubbing his eyes.

"Oh, Henry!" She threw her paws around him. But he pulled back at once.

"What are you doing down here?" said Mona. "Did you hear, see, smell . . . ?"

"Uh-huh," he sniffled. "You . . . don't want me. I don't belong here. . . ."

Right away she knew he wasn't hiding from the owls. He was hiding from her!

Henry must have come down here right after he heard the fight between her and Tilly. Before she could say anything, however, he gave an extra-big sniffle. "I'm just trying . . . trying my best. . . .

Maybe I shouldn't be here. Maybe I should go back to Hood's."

"Oh." Mona gulped. "You heard me talking to Tilly, didn't you?"

He nodded and sniffled. "I know you don't want me here. I don't belong."

It struck her how his words sounded like her own, like the conversation she had in the fall with Tilly when *she* was new to the Heartwood, and Tilly was treating her badly. Tilly was worried she would lose her job to Mona and hadn't made Mona feel welcome. Mona wasn't scared she'd lose her job to Henry, but she was afraid of losing something.

She moved closer to the squirrel. There wasn't much space, but enough. Room for two.

"I'm sorry for what I said. Really, Henry. I . . . I was just afraid."

"Afraid?" he squeaked.

"Yes," said Mona. "Afraid of losing my place here . . . afraid everyone liked you better than me." She looked at the little squirrel.

"But everyone LOVES you!" said Henry, astonished. "All the guests know your name. Ms. Prickles says you're good with your paws. Gilles says you have the best ideas, and Tilly wishes her heart was as big as yours."

"Really?" said Mona, smiling. But the smile quickly disappeared. "Tilly . . ." Mona's voice caught.

"What's the matter?" said Henry.

"Tilly's trapped outside because . . ."

Henry's eyes widened.

Mona didn't want to scare him; still, he needed to know the truth.

"Owls have attacked the Heartwood, Henry."

Henry's tail exploded into a poof. "OWLS?" he cried. "Tilly's outside and there are OWLS?!"

"Not just Tilly," said Mona.

Henry started up the stairs. "Come on, Mona. We have to do something. We HAVE to!"

Mona shook her head. "It won't be easy. We can't trick them away like the wolves or face them like the snowstorm. We'd need an army to attack the owls. But every . . . everyone else is stuck under the stage."

She almost felt hopeless again, but Henry looked at her.

"Not everyone," said Henry. "Not me. And aren't the . . ."

"The bees," Mona finished for him.

There *was* an army—a squadron—in the hotel. A squadron with stingers.

Mona and Henry climbed out of the secret room and hurried up the stairs to the hive room, in the hollow knot. The hotel was so quiet it was frightening. The higher they climbed, the tighter Henry clasped her paw, and she understood why. Mona could feel the danger, coursing through the tree, thicker than sap.

When at last they reached the sticky hallway, Mona knocked on the tiny door.

"We are off duty and packing," came the captain's voice from within. "Leave us be."

"It's Mona the maid. Please, Captain, it's an emergency."

The door opened, and Captain Ruby looked up at her. Mona could see, behind the captain, the hollow chamber that was built into the knot in the tree. All the honeycombs were empty. The bees were buzzing loudly behind the captain, arguing about where to go next. They must have been arguing for a while and had not heard the attack.

"I am serious when I say we are leaving," said the captain.

"You can't," cried Mona. "We need your help."

"With honey production?" said the captain.

"No, with protection, not production," said Mona. "Owls. *Owls* have attacked the Heartwood."

"BZZT!" Immediately, Captain Ruby sprang to attention. The bees stopped arguing and were on the alert. "Owls! I heard some shrieks but assumed that was part of the festivities. That explains it. Our flank *was* exposed. What of your defense?"

"We don't have any," said Mona. "We only have Tony to warn us. But he's stuck under the stage in the courtyard." As she described everything that had happened, the captain paced.

"Owls, you say. More than one? Owls don't usually attack in squadrons. This is highly unusual. I could lead a counterattack but . . ."

"But what?" asked Mona. "Buts" were never good when it came to plans.

"Their feathers are thick. Our stingers might get stuck."

Mona gulped. "So you can't attack?"

"No, I didn't say that. I doubt we'd need to sting them; a good swarm would scare them away. Especially a precise, persistent formation that stays with them until they leave. I could lead that type of counterattack, but in the dark it is difficult to maneuver. Or even find the owls. We must wait until daybreak. . . ."

"We can't," said Mona. "By daybreak it'll be too late."

Just then, to prove her point, there was another shriek. The unmistakable shriek of the Robinsons, louder than it had ever been before.

Henry tugged Mona's paw. But Mona was lost in thought.

"What about lanterns?" she suggested.

The captain shook her head. "We can't carry lanterns. They will weigh us down. No, we must find another way. . . ."

Henry tugged Mona's paw again.

 132

"What is it, Henry?" she asked.

"The fireflies," he said. "The fireflies are here, too. *They* could light up the sky, Mona. They could do it. I know they could."

"Henry, that's it!" said Mona.

But the captain didn't seem to think so. "Florian and the Flares? I could never work with those fireflies!"

To Mona's dismay, the fireflies didn't want to work with the bees either. Mona and Henry gathered both groups in the lobby, on the rug in front of the fireplace.

"We're artists. We're not trained for this," said Florian. His light trembled. "You are. You always boast you have the best formations. Isn't this your chance?"

"Believe me, I'd rather we attack on our own," the captain buzzed back.

Every second wasted felt like a whole season.

Mona couldn't hear any more shrieks outside, but silence was almost worse. She didn't know what might be happening.

"Please," said Mona. "We have to save everyone. We have to save the Heartwood!" She tried to think of how the captain would say it, but all she could think of was, "If we work together, we stand a chance."

Captain Ruby paused. "I see the makings of a captain in you, Mona. And in time of need, a good captain does what she must, but . . . it's not like they know the Encircle Maneuver."

"You mean Ring Around the Treetop? Of course we do," said Florian. "It's one of our favorites."

"You do?" The captain looked surprised. "What about Thread the Needle?"

Florian and his troupe nodded.

"Blast Off?"

"Do you mean a sudden burst of flight? That's what we call a Flash of Fire," said the firefly. "We've done that a thousand times. We could perform it in our sleep." He hesitated, then at last said, "I suppose we *are* trained. I suppose——"

"Just this once . . ." interrupted Captain Ruby.

"We *can* work together," they finished at the same time.

"Oh, thank you," cried Mona.

"Don't thank us yet," said the captain. "The night is far from over. The real battle has yet to begin."

Firefly Works

All was silent on the stargazing balcony, except for the thump of Mona's heart and the soft skittering as a few fireflies flew up to the top branches to scout out the owls.

Once the fireflies found the owls, they'd give a signal, and the rest of the troupe would join them. Then the bees would swarm.

Mona huddled with Henry, safe in the doorway. The cluster of lanterns lit the balcony like a tiny moon. But in the sky, the real moon was hidden by clouds. Around and above them the darkness was thick and threatening.

Henry clutched Mona's paw tightly.

"You can go below," whispered Mona.

"Nuh-uh," said Henry. "I want to stay with you."

Mona was glad. She wanted him there as well.

In the shadows at the side of the balcony, Captain Ruby and her squadron, and Florian and his troupe, waited in position. Would the scouts find the owls? And if they did, would the plan work? Would the bees scare them away?

Mona's worrying grew until, through a break in the black branches above . . .

BLINK, BLINK!

The signal.

It all happened in a heartbeat.

The sky lit up and buzzing filled the air. First the bees flew in a single giant V. Then they split into smaller Vs to target the enemies, and the attack began.

SCREEECH!

The owls shot into the air.

The fireflies flashed, the bees swarmed—was that Ring Around the Treetop or Flash of Fire?—and the owls screeched in surprise and dismay. Firefly works, indeed! The attack was spectacular. Never had such a sight been seen in the skies over Fernwood Forest. In a swirl of feathers, the owls swooped off into the night. First one, then two, then three.

"They did it!" cried Henry, now clearly more excited than scared. "Look! Captain Ruby is coming back!"

But what about the fourth owl? It must have flown off, too. Mona just hadn't seen it.

Captain Ruby landed in front of Mona and Henry. The rest of her squadron and the fireflies followed. They were all excited, giving one another buzzes and blinks of congratulations.

"Mission complete!" announced the captain. "I'm here to report our counterattack has been

effective! Thanks to the Flares. Top-notch, those fireflies."

"Your formations are top-notch, too," said Florian, alighting next to the bee. "I've never seen Flash of Fire—I mean, Blast Off—performed so well."

"Did all the owls . . ." Mona searched for the word.

"Retreat?" replied Captain Ruby. "Indeed." She turned to Florian. "I suppose our formations ARE full of feeling. They make the enemy feel scared."

"Truth be told, I felt a little scared myself," said Florian.

The captain buzzed. "Me too. Though don't tell my squadron." And this time, she chuckled.

"But . . ." Mona tried again. The bees and fireflies weren't letting Mona get a word in once more—this time not because they were arguing, but because they were complimenting one another.

"Speaking of fear," said the captain, "we must

tell the staff and guests what has happened. We don't want them to be afraid a moment longer." Captain Ruby signaled and was joined this time by not only her squadron but the Flares as well. Together, they flew away, down off the balcony, toward the stage.

They must be sure all the owls are gone, thought Mona, relieved.

Until she heard Florian's and Ruby's voices, faintly in the distance.

"You just reinvented the Bye-Bye-Blink!" Florian said.

"Bye-bye indeed!" said the captain. "We won't be seeing those three owls for a long time."

Three! They had only scared away *three* owls— not four! There *was* still one left. She was sure she told them there were four. But she couldn't remember. And now it didn't matter. If everyone came out from under the stage and there was an owl waiting above . . .

"Wait, Captain!" Mona cried, tugging her paw from Henry's.

"What's going on?" asked Henry, startled.

There was no time to explain.

"You stay here!" said Mona.

"But . . ." Henry's tail bristled.

Mona scurried into the darkness. "Wait!" she cried, louder this time.

But only silence answered her. She couldn't even hear the buzzing of the bees.

Still, she tried to call one last time, but her voice came out as a squeak.

Her tail and whiskers trembled, and her fur stood on end. The wood below her paws was cold. She could feel the light from the cluster of lanterns on her back, like the stare of a big blazing eye. It made her shiver. And she knew—it wasn't just the lights. There was an eye—a real eye staring at her.

It was the fourth owl, in the branches above.

He was waiting. Waiting for *her*.

"YOU!" came a low hoot.

Mona spun around. Claws extended, one eye glowing, the other a mass of scars, the owl swooped down upon Mona.

She dove across the balcony, out of reach of the owl, safe for the moment. But she kept sliding, sliding, right to the balcony's edge. She grasped for the railing and grabbed it, just in time.

The owl landed.

"YOU," he called, furiously snapping his beak. "YOU." The owl began to make his way oh-so-slowly toward her. His claws scraped against the wood. If only the fireflies and bees hadn't left!

"Help!" Mona wanted to cry, but her voice was stuck in her throat.

The owl's eye glowed brighter.

"YOU!" It was the hooting cry that marked the end of many a mouse's life.

Mona shook. There was nowhere left to go. Only branches and air loomed below her.

"YOU!" The owl lunged at Mona.

TWEET!

It happened in an instant. The owl swiveled his head toward the sound of Henry's whistle. Suddenly, he was surrounded by fireflies and bees.

He turned away from Mona, but as he did so, his wing grazed her side, and she lost her grip.

Was that Captain Ruby she saw in the darkness? And Henry, too?

It was all a blur as she fell down, down, down. . . .

MONA MENDS

Mona groaned.

Her head ached. Her tail ached. But most of all, one of her paws ached—so much she didn't think she'd ever be able to walk on it again.

Slowly she opened her eyes. She was in the nicest and biggest bed imaginable. She had fluffed its feathers before, but never slept in it. It was the bed in the penthouse suite. Was she dreaming?

Sunlight streamed through the window. How long had she been sleeping? How did she get here? What had happened? Was everyone okay?

"Mona! You're awake."

It was Tilly.

Mona wasn't dreaming. Tilly was sitting beside the bed. Her fur was a mess. The bow hung lop-sided between her ears, and her face was all matted, as if she'd been crying.

Mona tried to sit, but Tilly said, "Don't move too quickly. You've twisted your paw."

Mona peeked under the blanket to see her left paw all bandaged up.

The red squirrel wiped her eyes, then crossed her arms. "Humph. What were you thinking, Mona? You almost got yourself killed! I KNEW you were going to try something like that. I knew it."

Tilly took a deep breath. "Oh, Mona. I . . . I was so scared for you, and for Henry. I didn't know where he was. But I couldn't leave, not just 'cause of the owls but 'cause I was trapped by quills. I mean, it's one thing to be stuck under a stage, and quite another to have porcupines on one side and hedgehogs on the other. Then I saw your face in the ballroom window. I knew . . . I knew you were okay. I hoped Henry was, too. But then . . ." She rolled her eyes. "Why do you always have to be a hero?"

"It wasn't just me . . . it was mostly the bees and fireflies and . . . Henry! Where is he? Is he okay?"

"I'm here." Henry peeked over the side of the bed.

"You saved my life," squeaked Mona.

"I just blew my whistle. I almost couldn't. I could barely breathe. I hate owls. I hate them!"

"It's okay," said Tilly. "They're gone now and won't be coming back." Tilly pulled her brother close.

Henry looked up at her. "It was Tilly who ran into the branches and rescued you, Mona. I've never seen her scurry so quickly, right out to the limbs."

"You did?" Mona asked Tilly.

"Of course I did," replied the squirrel softly. "I'd do anything for you. You're my best friend."

It was the nicest thing Tilly had ever said.

"That's the only kind of best that matters," added Mona. And it was true. She felt warm and happy all over. The grump was gone.

"Okay, okay," said Tilly with a humph. "We're getting as sappy as the tree."

"Not as sappy as Ms. Prickles. She even made sap soup yesterday, and it was icky," said Henry.

"What do you mean?" asked Mona.

"Oh boy," said Tilly. "Ms. Prickles is in love."

"What?!" cried Mona. "With who?"

"Can you believe it? It's one of the guests," said Tilly. "I guess they had been sweet on each other years ago when he came to the hotel, but she had refused him. Ms. Prickles said she always regretted it. When he saw the Splash flyer with 'Prickles's

Petal Pastries' on it, he knew she still worked here and decided to come and try one last time to win her over. He was planning on talking to her at once, but lost his nerve. . . . Ms. Prickles showed me where he carved a heart for her on the tree trunk and also a poem he wrote for her . . ."

"In the guest book," finished Mona, remembering the one that said, "*Seedcakes warm, soufflés soft, you'll be with me in my thoughts.—Q.*"

Q was Mr. Quillson. Mr. Quillson wasn't a spy. He was in love with the Heartwood's cook!

"How do you . . . never mind," said Tilly. "Speaking of guest books, that reminds me. One of the guests wanted me to give this to you when you woke up."

"I thought staff weren't allowed to get gifts from guests."

"Well, staff aren't allowed to sleep in guest rooms either," Tilly teased.

Mona smiled as Tilly handed over the gift. It

was a book—a guest book. Several pages were marked with blades of grass.

"I'm sorry I didn't get a chance to read the books with you," said Tilly. "Apparently this guest is a speed reader. He was worried he read the books too fast the first time. He reread them and found these entries. He wanted to stay and show you them himself, but he had to go on his way. It takes him a long time to get anywhere since he's a snail."

Skim, thought Mona. Her heart beat fast as she opened the book to the first blade of grass and began to read.

The Heartwood Hotel was a wonderful place for a mole like myself to make art. The stay was even more productive than I expected thanks to the helpful suggestions of two mice guests I befriended.
—Mr. Moltisse

Two mice. Her parents!

Mona flipped to the next bookmark.

Twelve kits are a handful. Thank whiskers for those two mice who were so great with them. What a surprise it was to discover we'd met a relative of theirs in the village.

—Mme. Hana the hedgehog

Her parents again. And relatives? Mona couldn't believe it. *What village? Where?*

She flipped the page to another entry, but this one had no writing.

There were two big ♥'s on the page, with eyes and whiskers drawn on them. It must have been drawn by those kits.

Tilly peeked over her shoulder.

"This isn't from your parents!" she said, disappointed. "Mona, I'm so sorry."

Mona shook her head. "Don't be, Tilly. My parents might not have written an entry, but they are part of so many. And . . . well." She was about to tell her about her relatives, but . . .

Instead of sharing the secret, she decided not to—at least not right away. Although most secrets were better shared, sometimes it was nice to hold on to something good that was just meant for you. At least for a moment. It felt like a whole family of mice had entered the room, filling it with warmth.

But it was another someone who actually filled the doorway. A big, whiskery, wonderful someone.

Mr. Heartwood!

16

THE HEARTWOOD HOP

Mr. Heartwood strode into the suite. His black-and-white fur was glossier than ever. Gone were his cap and cardigan, and the keys were back around his neck. Was it Mona's imagination, or was there a new key added to the collection? Instead of having a heart-shaped top, however, this key was wavy and shaped like a raindrop.

The big badger gestured to the guest book Mona was reading. "A single guest's praise outdoes ten who complain. But I'd rather no praise than a staff member in pain." His eyes crinkled with concern. "When I heard what had happened, I hurried back. I didn't mean to be gone so long. How are you feeling, Miss Mouse?"

"I'm fine, Mr. Heartwood," said Mona, though she *was* feeling very tired.

"I'm glad to hear it," he replied. "Though I am not glad to hear there were owls at the hotel."

"It was because of the Splash. Are . . . are we in trouble?" stammered Henry.

Mr. Heartwood was serious for a moment before he said, "We all make mistakes, but it's pointless to blame. Still, safety was forgotten and that's a great shame. I won't be leaving the hotel again anytime soon. I wanted to go to the grand opening, but I have decided not to."

Even though they weren't in trouble, Mona felt bad that they had let Mr. Heartwood down. And now he had to change his plans because of what had happened. She hoped there would be another chance later to prove they could look after the hotel and wanted to say so, when Henry piped:

"Grand opening of what?"

Mr. Heartwood held out the new wavy key. "My dear friend I was visiting is starting a new hotel, Beaver Lodge, for water animals."

Could it be? The "splashy" hotel was a hotel for water animals!

"*That's* the hotel we were so worried about?" cried Tilly, who clearly hadn't heard this news either.

"Indeed," said Mr. Heartwood. "Benjamin wanted my help organizing it, and I thought it would be a good chance to relax. Work for one is another's fun. And there is nothing like helping a friend. I would have told you all, but Benjamin wished that I keep it secret, in case it didn't work out. But oh, how it has! The Beaver Lodge truly will change the flow of Fernwood, for it requires a new dam at the top of the stream."

"That's not competition," cried Tilly. "Not at all!"

"But even if it was another forest hotel, it wouldn't be competition," said Mona, glancing over at Henry. "Right, Mr. Heartwood?"

Mr. Heartwood nodded. "As long as we stick to what we do best, a humble hotel meant for rest, then we are sure to have plenty of guests. . . ."

It was a three-part rhyme.

Mr. Heartwood was back and in fine form!

As he began to describe the hotel, from its otter manager to its muskrat maids, Mona couldn't help but feel her eyes grow heavier and heavier. Before she knew it, she drifted off, dreaming of the new hotel with its bulrush blankets and lily-pad pillows and watery beds that rocked you in the waves. But instead of muskrat or minnow maids, there were mice, with whiskers that tickled her gently as they sang her to sleep.

Mona stayed in the penthouse for the whole week. Mr. Heartwood insisted. She felt as pampered as a guest! Everyone was really nice to her. Except sometimes Tilly, who humphed, "Really, how long does it take for a paw to heal? It's impossible to get everything cleaned without you. I don't know what I did before you were here." Still, Tilly found time to sew a new heart on Mona's apron.

Henry was always there, running errands for Mona, whether she wanted him to or not. Mostly she did.

Then one day he announced proudly: "Mr. Heartwood's given me a job! I'm the Heartwood bellhop. At first I told him hopping's for rabbits and frogs. But he said a bellhop can be anyone. Anyone who's good at running errands. And I've been running so many!"

"You'll do a great job," said Mona. Even if it meant he'd be asking her lots of questions, she didn't mind.

"Thanks!" said Henry, hopping almost as high as a rabbit, he was so excited.

Soon Mona was hopping, too, around the room on a twig crutch. The only place she didn't go was out onto the penthouse balcony. Although she didn't admit it to anyone, she was scared. The penthouse balcony was smaller than the stargazing one but otherwise very similar. Every time Mona looked out at it, she thought of the owl—and his big blazing eye.

Even so, from the balcony window, she could see the courtyard. Gone were the eggs, the flowers, the stage. Instead, it was a plain mossy area once more, framed with blackberries and dotted with mushroom-cap seats, just the way Mona liked it. Until she didn't need crutches, however, it would be tricky for Mona to go down all the Heartwood stairs. So that's why Mr. Heartwood decided to have the Heartwood Hop in the penthouse instead of in the ballroom. They couldn't end spring, he declared, without a proper Heartwood fling. A humble one, this time.

Humble—and perfect.

There was music in the living room. No bands, just a single frog and one raccoon, playing tunes together. Gilles seemed slightly subdued both in color and in mood as he gave out medals to Captain Ruby and Florian for their bravery, but no other prizes. It was his last task as manager. Afterward, Mona saw him take off his badge and put it in his pocket. Mona felt a little bad for him, but then she saw Mrs. Higgins put her paw on his shoulder. "A good manager doesn't need a show, only quiet skill, which you have," said Mrs. Higgins. It was the nicest way of saying "I told you so" that Mona had ever heard.

The dining room was filled with Ms. Prickles's food, of which Mr. Quillson ate the most (but Tilly and Henry, close seconds).

There were only a few guests invited. Skim would have been one of them, but he was already on his way to the water hotel. It turned out his birthday booking was for the grand opening. He would have been early, but now, as long as he didn't get confused again, he'd be right on time.

The Robinsons were there, though, with their baby bird, who had hatched at last. Underneath the stage, in fact. That had been why Mrs. Robinson had shrieked so loudly in the dark: her baby had been born. The little chick was mostly pink and gray, but her eyes were already open.

"What's her name?" asked Mona, balanced on her crutch in the dining room, munching a seedcake.

"Ruby," said Mrs. Robinson proudly.

"Florian—if it was a boy," added Mr. Robinson. "We were thinking of naming her Mona, but our little chick shall grow to be red-chested, of course. . . ."

"Of course," said Mona. "Ruby is a really nice—"

A loud *CRASH* interrupted Mona.

"Oops!" cried Mrs. Robinson.

"Not again!" sighed Mr. Robinson. Baby Ruby had somehow pulled a platter off the table and seed-cakes rained down on her little fluffy head, nearly burying her. Instead of making a peep, she began to peck at the seeds.

"No, Ruby, don't eat those," said Mrs. Robinson.

Mr. Robinson added, "You're not on solid food yet, just regurgitated worms."

Baby Ruby was a wingful. And as fearless as Captain Ruby.

Come to think of it, where was Captain Ruby? Mona glanced over at the doorway to the balcony. Probably outside again. The bees had decided to stay at the Heartwood after all. Not just stay: Captain Ruby, along with Florian and Tony, had been patrolling the forest around the Heartwood all week, and so far there had been no sign of any owls.

Still . . .

Mona shivered.

Then she noticed Henry. He was standing by the doorway, staring outside. His tail was all puffed up. Mona hopped closer, trying to see what he was looking at.

But there was no one on the balcony. Only the dark sky, the stars, and the oak leaves.

"Henry's scared to go outside," explained Tilly, coming up behind Mona. "After what happened . . ."

"Me too," said Mona. "But maybe if there's three of us, it won't be so scary."

Henry nodded.

And so, holding paws, the three of them stepped out.

The night was still and quiet, the party a happy hum behind them. Below, the forest was a sea of waving treetops, bathed in the moon's honey glow. Above, the stars glittered like faraway fireflies, while much closer, real fireflies glittered as they flew with the bees around and around the hotel.

The air was sweet and warm. Mona's heart felt full. Yet she knew now there was plenty of room for whatever—or whomever—summer might bring.

"It's not scary," said Henry. "It's . . ."

"Hearthopping," said Mona.

It wasn't a real word, but it bounced from her in the moment, and it felt just right.

"Hearthopping?" Tilly's eyebrows rose.

"Sometimes no words will do," Mona explained, "except for ones you make anew."

Tilly rolled her eyes. "Oh, Mona, you sound *just* like Mr. Heartwood."

Mona couldn't feel prouder.

THE PINECONE PRESS: NEWS! NEWS! NEWS!

Beaver Lodge Opens with a Splash

Yesterday, Beaver Lodge, a new hotel, opened in the pond at the edge of Fernwood Forest. The event was exciting for all those who splashed by. Catering specifically to  aquatic folk, the hotel features a well-marked special underwater entrance, as well as mudrooms for frogs, an exercise room for energetic otters, and rooms on the roof for water striders. There are even day-lounge alcoves for fish who are looking to take a protected noon snooze.

Mr. Benjamin Banks, the hotel's owner, was inspired by his good friend Mr. Heartwood, owner of the five-acorn

Heartwood Hotel, which was featured in our fall issue. "Like the Heartwood," said Mr. Benjamin, "we are adopting the motto *We live by* 'Protect and Respect,' *not by* 'Tooth and Claw,' and so we plan on serving only vegetation in our restaurant."

Waterweed stew, lily-pad pâté, and bark biscuits are featured items on the menu. The hotel promises impeccable service, with muskrat maids for above water and minnow maids for below. They even offer a shallow beach area for land creatures to visit with their gilled friends. A welcome addition to our forest, this hotel is sure to be a draw for creatures traveling by stream and looking for a place to stay. An official review, along with the acorn rating, will come once the hotel is up and flowing.

IN OTHER NEWS: Petunia Prickles will be joining paws with Quentin Quillson, Midsummer Day, at the Heartwood Hotel. By invitation only.

Acknowledgments

So many wonderful people—family, friends, and colleagues—have made room for me and my stories in their lives. Thank you to my dad, my mom, my brother, and Marie, and my grandparents, who watch over me; as well as my friends, including the Inkslingers (Tanya Lloyd Kyi, Rachelle Delaney, Christy Goezern, Shannon Ozirny, Lori Sherritt-Fleming, and Maryn Quarless), Lee Edward Fodi, Sara Gillingham, and Vikki Vansickle. Thank you to my amazing editors, Rotem Moscovich and Suzanne Sutherland, and to the fantastic teams at Disney Hyperion and HarperCollins Canada, and to the brilliant artist Stephanie Graegin. Thank you to my wonderful agent, Emily van Beek; my dear husband, Luke Spence Byrd; and the incredible Tiffany Stone, who practically lives at the Heartwood Hotel with me when I'm writing about it.

Don't miss the next book in the series!